Total Control

ISBN. 979 870 056 1471

TOTAL CONTROL

Chapter one.

The White House. Washington D.C.

Stewart Phillips had expected to find a lot of sightseers outside the White House. It was a warm day and there were a few groups admiring the building but they were mainly schoolchildren. Stewart and his work colleague Ray Wheeler had been summoned by the President to attend a meeting and they both knew this would be an important visit to the White House. Like most citizens of the United States he was aware of who the President is and what he looks like but to be attending a meeting with the great man was just a bit special. After very close scrutiny of their identities including iris and fingerprint checks a very smartly dressed aide had escorted them from the entrance through what seemed to Stewart to be the offices where all the work was carried out. They were shown into a comfortable and informal room which contained a large table surrounded by chairs and an informal seating area with a low coffee table. On the coffee table was a tray and the aide told them to help themselves to coffee and biscuits and that the President would be with them very soon. Ray offered to pour while Stewart looked around and chose the nearest chair to sit down.

Stewart looked at Ray and they both smiled, they were still finding it incredible that they were inside the White House, calmly drinking coffee and waiting to meet the President of the United States.

They were both Boeing employees who were involved in developing top secret systems and had been summoned to explain what they did at work; it was as simple as that. Both of them had taken care with their appearances, wearing what Stewart laughing called his funeral or wedding attire and did not really understand why he had chosen to wear a pair of socks that were the same colour as his tie. Maybe some of his brothers' dress sense was beginning to rub off on him after all this time.

His thoughts were interrupted by a very smart marine who opened the door and announced, "The President of the United States of America." Stewart half expected to hear the sound of 'Hail to the Chief' as he stood up to attention. The President strode into the room followed by two very large men who were introduced as "my security detail". The President apologised for keeping them waiting and explained his previous meeting had overrun. He saw the tray and asked if there was any more coffee to which Ray replied, "certainly sir, how do you take it?"

"Thanks, little milk and no sugar will be just fine. Please sit down and let us get straight to the purpose of the meeting. Tell me about this software that you have been working on. I don't want the technical details, I assume you have got that right, I just need to know it's purpose and how effective it can be."

Ray Wheeler responded first because he oversaw the project. Stewart was puzzled because he thought the President knew about every project and sanctioned every defence or military initiative.

"Sir, we have been working alongside the military on an offensive weapon, the software originated as a defence against hijacking. Originally more than five hundred programmers were involved who did the bulk of the work. The purpose of the software was changed so that it could be used as a weapon, we were ideally suited to make those changes due to our experience with controlling drones and missiles. In its original form the software could take control of a hijacked aircraft, shut down all communications and fly the aircraft to a suitable airfield where is could be landed safely and be secured. It has never been used for that purpose despite there being several opportunities."

"Why was that?"

"The system is operated by a government department and that department along with the military decided that it had more value as a weapon."

"Who made that decision, it certainly was not me?"

"No idea Sir, we are not involved in that sort of decision."

"Carry on."

"We were working in parallel with other programmers who were designing software for unmanned freighter and passenger aircraft."

The President groaned, "Heaven forbid. I do not think I could board Airforce One if there were no pilots in the cockpit."

Stewart smiled." It sounds horrific but it's not."

Ray continued.

"The version of software that we are working on can take control of any aircraft on a routine flight without assistance from the flight crew or anyone else on board and can then be flown into designated targets. Numerous planes can be controlled at any one time and sent to different locations."

The President looked worried, "Killing all the people on board?"

"Afraid so Sir but consider that could be five hundred souls but the objective is to deter a nuclear strike which could kill hundreds of thousands."

"It is to be used as a deterrent?"

"Exactly, it gives the United States the same control as we had when we were the only country with nuclear weapons."

The President was taking it all in. "All we have to do is modify all the airliners?"

"Not so, most airliners are already fitted with this software, they are supplied that way as standard."

"Can the software be de-activated or removed?"

"It's not possible, the aircraft wouldn't fly, and we would know if any attempt was being made to interfere or alter the system."

"How could you stop that?"

"Someone would talk to the culprits and if they did not listen, they would have an unexpected visitor at the place that is carrying out the work."

"Are there many airliners that are equipped with the modified software?"

"More than twenty thousand."

"Are they an effective weapon?"

"You saw what happened to the World Towers when they were hit by aircraft."

The President nodded.

"What defence is there against such an attack?

"None, if an aircraft took off from Ronald Reagan Airport, which is five miles from here and control was taken over as soon as it was airborne it would be here in two minutes. Missiles and fighters would not help and even if they could destroy the aircraft in the air the fuel and debris would be scattered over Washington. If one is taking off right now, I would barely have time to shake hands and say goodbye."

"Frightening."

"Once control is taken over the aircraft can no longer be controlled by anyone on board." Ray paused, "If for example the crew had been killed or injured and maybe the passengers then we can safely bring the aircraft down to a secure landing place. Everything is operational now."

The President thought for a moment before continuing. "This system must remain solely under the control of the United States. Total control. Already there will be countries that want to take that control away from us. Large countries such as China and Russia will be at the front of the queue, while smaller but nuclear armed countries such as North Korea will also be looking at it. Our biggest concerns are smaller irrational countries and terrorist organisations."

The President had understood the danger and he continued. "Many of those are run by madmen. What do they need to take over the control of an aircraft?"

"Very little, the system can be controlled from a standard computer."

"Ok, you've made your point. Is that really all they would need?"

"They would also need someone who had been trained to operate the system and knows how to control an aircraft. Stewart and I are the only two people who understand everything. Even the operators for the anti-hijack system are not able to operate this modified system, they still need an input from the cockpit of the plane they want to control."

The President went silent for a while. "But I have been told that you have a problem. If I understand this correctly both of you are in an extremely dangerous situation."

"We are but…"

The President interrupted. "There is no but about it you need to be protected at all cost and by protecting you we will protect this country and the world."

The President got up from his chair and Stewart and Ray stood up. "I want you to continue to work on solving the current issue, anything you require will be available on my direct orders. I want to thank you for taking the time to explain this system to me and I want you to make it a priority that we, the United States have total control. Is that understood?"

Ray and Stewart replied in unison. "Understood, we will do everything to make sure the system is secure."

Chapter Two.

Two years earlier, Aberdeen, Washington State. USA.

It was a bright sunny day, just the weather for being in the garden. His nearest neighbour obviously thought so and raised his arm.

"Morning Stewart, I'm sorry to hear about your father."

The two houses were separated by a low wooden fence and a line of bushes. He nodded acknowledgement; the man was always friendly, but he did not know his name. He was middle aged, and he had heard a woman's voice but had not seen her. They had moved in a month ago and he must have learned his name from his father who spent a lot of time gardening. In fact, his father spent little time inside the house unlike himself who spent most of his time indoors at his apartment at Renton near to where he worked. If he were truthful with himself, he would have to admit to being lonely. Today he was in effect saying goodbye to his father Albert, the house, the garden and really wanted to take it all in. Preferably without having to talk to his neighbour, the man seemed to realise this and moved away without speaking again.

His chair and table were in a shaded part of the garden and Stewart set his coffee down and lowered himself into the chair. Looking slowly around him taking in the trees and bushes that he had planted with his father his mind slipped back to those early days of his childhood. His parents had left Scotland for a new life in Canada; they were escaping war torn Britain which even twenty years after the war ended was still struggling. Unfortunately, soon after arriving they had decided that it was not the place for them and had driven south into the United States, that was in 1966. They settled in Aberdeen which was about two hundred miles south of the border. When questioned why they had chosen Aberdeen his father always said it was because the town, and it was a small town then, did not have a decent carpentry business and he was a carpenter. Everybody realised that the real reason was that he had been born in Aberdeen, Scotland and he was now living in Aberdeen, USA. He was not on his own as there were a lot of Scots living there and, of course, that was why the town was called Aberdeen; the original settlers who had named it were Scots. His mother had often said that the Aberdeen where they were living was nothing like the one, they had left behind in Scotland. The only similarity was that they were both ports.

His father had moved with his wife Rose, Stewart's mother, into a rented house and he had started work for a local joinery company. They made window frames, door frames and doors; he often spoke of the big step when he was moved onto doors. There was a wide selection, unlike door frames which he had been making since the day he started at the factory. Two years after arriving in Aberdeen they found this house on the outskirts of town, the house where Stewart was sitting in the garden, which was now surrounded by the ever-expanding town. One of the first improvements his father had made was to build a large shed in the garden where he could build furniture for their new home. As the area expanded, he was making furniture for his neighbours and then for customers far and wide and the shed grew and Phillips Bespoke Joinery was founded. Within a few years the number of employees had reached ten, so he bought a commercial business in town that sold paint and extended the property to accommodate twenty joiners. He sold the paint business and concentrated on joinery which because of its high quality products went from strength to strength. It was a successful business.

Rose had presented him with twin boys, Alistair and Stewart who were almost identical, this was confusing when they started school. Now they were both in their forties and Stewart put his head back as he recalled the good times they had had over the years, tears flowed, and he wiped them with his shirt sleeve.

They had enrolled at Aberdeen High School in the same class and had shown a competitive streak which was always good humoured. Albert their father had always known that the joinery business was not for them and did not have expectations of either of them taking it over. It was a shock for all concerned when they chose to continue their education at different universities. Alistair went to New York to study economics while Stewart went to Embay-Riddle Aeronautical University at Renton. This was less than one hundred and fifty miles away which meant that he was often at home at Aberdeen unlike Alistair who had to make a big effort to cross the country resulting in their mother often commenting that she rarely saw him. Stewart had talked to Alistair about it but he had explained that he was studying economics and his future after qualifying was in New York. Alistair accepted that his brother, who was studying computer technology as it applied to aviation, was in the best place for his future.

The largest aircraft manufacturer in the world was 'just up the road' at Everett. The university course that Stewart had qualified for was sponsored by Boeing, but that did not mean he was duty bound to work for them. There were aircraft manufacturers all over the country and exciting opportunities were everywhere. Stewart even considered the United Kingdom as a possible place to work; disappointingly Aberdeen in Scotland did not have any aviation opportunities. In the end the brothers went on their predicted ways. Alistair went to work for a global organisation that advised companies on their financial strategy. Stewart joined Boeing in their software development group at an extremely exciting time as new ideas were constantly emerging.

It was a shock to them when their mother died; she had always been healthy but died in her sleep. She was sixty and had been married for forty years. Their father had telephoned both sons and Stewart had been home within a couple of hours, but Alistair took three days and only just made the funeral. They had a heated discussion, a rare occurrence, but Stewart thought that there was nothing more urgent than comforting their father who was burying his wife. In the months that followed he noticed he was running the business down and Albert admitted that he was trying to sell it. Eventually four of his employees took it over and he retired, he was sixty-one years old and felt it was time to retire and look after his garden.

Stewart had visited Alistair a couple of times in New York and within four years was taken to the offices of Alistair Phillips Incorporated. His company was doing very well and had all the signs of growing further, a swish apartment on Lexington Avenue and a glamorous girlfriend were the signs of his personal success. Stewart loved everything to do with airplanes and while at University he joined the gliding club and gained his pilot's license. On his first day working for Boeing at their base at Everett he had been introduced to several software developers and joined a team in a medium sized building that was close to the production buildings. Every week he watched new aircraft emerging from production, at that stage they were unpainted, and they were immediately test flown before disappearing to the paint shop. Yet another couple of days passed before they reappeared resplendent in the colours of the airline that had bought them. From his office window he could see aircraft that were parked out awaiting collection by the airline pilots.

It was amazing, they appeared out of the assembly building and in less than ten days they were taxying out and disappeared. When he had joined the company, he had been thrilled at the prospect of working on airplanes but quickly learned that he would rarely get close to one. Their building was an old one but had been renovated to a high standard for the 'software guys'. He mentioned this to one of his workmates.
"Haven't you figured it out yet? "
Stewart had to admit he was intrigued.
"Well airplanes are our main business and will always be, but the stuff we are working on over here is the future and has to be protected. Have you not noticed the high level of security? We are tucked away in our own building and we don't mix with production over there." He nodded towards the big production building. "And they don't come over here and mix with us."
Stewart commented. "But the public go on guided tours over there; all over the facility I could join one of those."
"You could, but unknown to you, there would be someone on that tour watching what you did and who you spoke to. You, we, are monitored all the time."
"I did not realise."
"Our work is valuable, not just to the company but to our country."
Stewart had to admit to himself that he had not noticed all this extra security and said so.
"How many programmers and software engineers are there in our building?"
"Never thought about it, lots."

"Try hundreds and every one of them locks the documents that they have been working on away every night."

Stewart had wondered about the safe at the end of his desk.

"At the moment you are working on routine stuff, when and if you graduate to the top-secret stuff you will find that you are monitored even more closely."

"Who are they concerned about?"

"Low level stuff attracts the interest of other aircraft makers but high-level stuff interests' other countries such as Russia and China and even European countries."

The brief discussion made him more aware of his situation.

Chapter Three.

Seattle.

Stewart was aware that he worked for a division of Boeing and not for the main company. He suspected that everybody worked for a separate division as the company was involved in every aspect of aviation. He readily accepted that they cooperated with Honeywell who were a major supplier to Boeing of navigation equipment. He also recognised that Jeppesen who produced all the aviation charts for the world were part of this union. What he found amazing was the extent of other cooperation agreements with companies such as Thales in France, Serco in England, and Freescale in the United States. They were major companies and innovators in the world of computing and software that applied to aviation. It was a shock when he learned that the entire division was moving to Washington DC, it did not make sense when he learned they were moving into a CIA building. That is until it was explained that they would be close to the White House and the Pentagon and he assumed the other companies, Thales, Serco, Freescale, and Jessops would be there. Obviously, some of their projects interested the government and the military.

When the move happened, he found that only part of their Renton operation moved and he was promoted to section leader, he was second in charge of software development for the 'unalterable auto pilot'. His apartment in Renton was basic and had one bedroom, it was student accommodation. But it was close to work in a suburb of Seattle and only about one hundred miles from his father. He would have liked his father to visit, to give him some company and as a break but the single bedroom was a problem. His promotion meant he could now afford to buy his own glider which he kept at a small airfield near Enumclaw and became an active member of the Puget Sound Soaring Association. His father Albert had settled into a life without Rose, but he was on his own, Stewart knew he had looked forward to him coming to visit at least for part of the weekend. Saturday morning was shopping day and they had lunch out, he had realised that he had become an important part of his father's life.

Then came the fatal day, he was in high spirits as he opened the back door and called out.

"Hi Dad, Its Stewart."

There was no reply, so he went through to the living room and found his father slumped in a chair, he was cold. He sat down beside him and talked about the garden, the house and Alistair. Albert did not say much and when Stewart stood up, he was sobbing, his dad had been a good man. He called the doctor who sent an ambulance to collect the body; it was only a body with no life in it. After the ambulance left, he called Alistair who promised to be there as soon as possible. Stewart sorted out his sofa bed so they could spend some time together and he and Alistair talked for hours.

Alastair asked Stewart if he was still flying his little kite and nodded when Stewart told him he had been up for a flight on that fateful Saturday and stayed up too long. He was later than usual getting to see Albert and wondered if he could have been there with him when he passed away. Alistair understood and tried to change the subject. "How are things progressing with that lovely lady you were dating? Shelia was it, no Sandra. Any movement there?"

Stewart sighed. "We parted company. I did think maybe we could have become closer and settled down but I began to realise that she resented the time I spent up in the glider and kept making remarks about how I never seemed to have time to go away with her. I went on a gliding holiday to Montana which was planned to be just for a week but the weather was great and the opportunities to fly were too good to pass and I stayed too long. She was not too happy when I got back as I think she had planned a trip away for us both but the crunch came when one weekend when I could not go flying, we ended up in a shopping mall. I suddenly found I was trying on trendy clothes and ended up spending far too much on stuff that I would never wear."

Alistair was laughing. "Well bro you never were a trendy dresser, look at you now, old worn-out jeans and a t-shirt that is only fit to be a duster, I bet all your spare cash goes on that kite!"

Stewart smiled. "You were always the well-dressed twin, that is how people could tell us apart. I bet your wardrobe is full of designer suits and lots of smart shirts. Talking of women how is that gorgeous red head, Katie if I remember, you two looked so good together?"

"Ah well, she was great. An asset at business dinners, witty, charming and I did begin to think we might be able to make something permanent. I got as far as talking about houses and family life and she told me that plan was not her idea of a future and she was off. I missed her for ages but was kept busy opening a new office in Washington DC. I was spending more time there as business was good and now, I live there most of the time and am thinking of selling my New York apartment and maybe even that part of the company."

"Well what a co-incidence. Part of the team I worked with relocated to Washington but I stayed here and have been promoted a few times but now they want me to go and take charge of a section in the Capitol. In fact that was what I was about to tell dad as I was concerned about who would keep an eye on him when I moved."

"That will be great, you can come and stay with me till you find a place. I have lots of room and space to store your stuff."

Stewart looked pleased. "We can become a pair of crusty old bachelors together."

"Steady on we are only in our forties."

"You know what I mean."

"Don't say anything else; we'll talk after the funeral."

Alistair did not head off after the funeral; in fact, he stayed for a few days while they sorted the house out and sold all the things that they did not want. They chatted about their lives and the differences and Alistair asked Stewart if he would be bringing his glider when he moved.

"Yes, I am due some leave so will hitch up the trailer to the old Ford F150 and enjoy a leisurely drive across. I will sell my furniture with the apartment and just bring my personal effects and those family items we have boxed up. Do you still hit a squash ball around the court and swim every day?"

Alistair replied that it was a way of getting rid of frustration and helped to keep him fit.

" Let me know when you are planning to arrive and we can finalise dad's affairs and get to know one another again."

Having had his last moments in the garden Stewart locked the house and dropped the keys off at the agent who was handling the sale. Sadly, it was the end of an era when the Phillips family had been part of the Aberdeen community, a sad day.

Chapter Four.

Washington. D.C.

Stewart sold his apartment quickly and a leaving date was agreed so he got out the maps and planned his journey across the country. Driving a large pickup truck towing a long trailer containing his glider meant he had to be sure of his parking place each night. Using his contacts through the Soaring Association he managed to arrange overnight halts at small airfields where he could be sure the trailer was safe and he could stay either on the airfield or at a nearby motel. He took the opportunity to call in and see the guys with whom he had been flying near Bozeman in Montana and left next morning a bit later than planned after a long night in the clubhouse. He could not miss the opportunity to visit the Dayton Aviation Heritage National Historic Park, Ohio and spent a whole day at the magnificent USAF museum admiring the aircraft on display. Stewart had made contact with the Eastern Soaring Centre based at the Grant County Airport, Petersburg West Virginia. This was the closest all year-round operations base serving the Washington DC area and set in the heart of the Appalachian Mountains. At just 50 miles west of where he would be living and working, he arrived to find a friendly group of enthusiasts who made him feel very welcome. He was soon enrolled as a new member and allocated a parking spot for his trailer and realised that the flying here was going to be a completely new experience. He had become knowledgeable about the weather patterns that formed over the Pacific and Puget sound but the Atlantic wind patterns and mountains would have to be respected until he understood them. He made arrangements to return once he was settled in and had time to unload his glider and maybe have some experience flights with an instructor before going up on his own again. Stewart felt quite excited as he drove into the capitol to find where he would be living and working.

Alistair had explained that for a while he had the two apartments as he had acquired the one in Washington for practical purposes. Stewart took this to mean that it paid him to be near to the headquarters of several government agencies. The apartment was in Alexandria, a district of Washington that was about five miles from the White House, a prime location. When Stewart arrived he found that it was a 'gated' community with security fences, and he had to sign in before he could get access through the gates. He expected to have to explain himself but was surprised that he was already on the list of visitors. Immediately he appreciated that Alistair had thought ahead. Inside the community were two low rise blocks, each one was five stories high but were entirely different designs. Both were modern design, and everything said quality. They were surrounded by superb gardens with ponds, trees, and spacious flower beds. This looked like a nice place to live. He found the block that housed Alistair's apartment without any difficulty. He noticed that there were four floors of apartments and the ground floor was office space. The offices belonged to Alistair

Phillips Incorporated and as Stewart pulled into a parking place Alistair was coming out of the front door to greet him.

"Great to see you. How was the trip? I will get in and show you where you can park in the underground garage." He gave Stewart instructions and directed him into a vacant place beside a dark blue Bentley Coupe. Stewart stopped the engine and remarked that his truck was a bit out of place here next to that beauty. Alistair admitted that it was his car and how much he enjoyed driving it, he explained that he had bought it in order to impress potential clients and had to admit to being very pleased. He told Stewart to grab his overnight bag while he arranged for the janitor to come and help load all his boxes into the lift. They soon had Stewarts meagre possessions stowed in a spare room and Alistair opened the door to a sumptuous bedroom and told Stewart that this would be his domain for as long as he needed.

"I have put in a couch, desk and a TV so you can be on your own if you want, you have your own facilities but will have to share the laundry, kitchen and lounge. Let me show you round."

There was a huge living room, a well-equipped kitchen and dining room, study, two more bedrooms, each with its own shower rooms and a cloakroom off the hallway. Alistair explained that as well as the underground garage the basement contained a swimming pool, gymnasium, and sauna. This magnificent top floor apartment had huge windows giving great views of the gardens below and the city skyline.

"Do you think this will be Ok for you?" Alistair seemed a little nervous.

"This is amazing, my bedroom is larger than my flat in Renton. I think I will be able to manage." Stewart replied as he hugged his brother. "It will be great to be together again and you can enjoy showing me this city and what goes on in the seat of power."

Over a takeaway dinner Alistair admitted that he owned the building and the second one nearby, well his company owned them as an investment. Stewart thought that Alistair seemed a bit lonely, maybe they were both lonely.

"I'll give you a job at Alistair Phillips Incorporated, on paper, and the share of the rent will come with the job."

"Steady on, what about Boeing?"

"That will be OK. You just need to tell them, don't let them find out later."

Stewart could see a good deal when it was offered.

"I'll check at HR and if they are OK with it, I'll stay here. Are all the apartments used by Alistair Phillips Incorporated?"

"Hell no, I need some rental income, there are sixteen that I rent out. It provides me with an income that covers all my living costs. I only work because I enjoy it. The tenants are all individuals and in some cases families with business connections here in Washington, they are all US citizens, some only appear from time to time. The offices on the ground floor in this block are used by my company but I also provide meeting rooms for the tenants of the apartments. Generally speaking, the public do not have access to them, during the day there are eight people working there who do not have access to the apartments above. The apartment below mine is occupied by a guy from Texas he is single and manages with a selection of young women who stay there. He's no trouble, I'll introduce you to him, and you'll get on with him."

Stewart avoided telling him that his tenants would be thoroughly checked out by the security services if he moved in. After a fun weekend relaxing and going on a guided tour of the city in Alistair's comfortable car Stewart was ready to go and meet the team of people with whom he would be working.

The CIA building where he was based was on the other side of the Potomac River from the White House and less than half a mile from the Pentagon. Unfortunately, it was under aircraft departing from Ronald Regan National Airport, as the building was well sound proofed noise was not an issue. He had very quickly got used to seeing departing aircraft a few hundred feet immediately overhead. Stewart was working alongside some of the same people who had been at the Seattle office but was a bit surprised to find that Ted McPherson had been one of the software engineers who had been moved to Washington. He was not a senior engineer and Stewart spoke to Ray about his surprise at finding him working there. Ray was also puzzled and said he always felt a bit uncomfortable when he found McPherson had entered the room. Stewart replied that he knew what he meant as most people made a comment when they came into the office, maybe just a quick hello or even a remark about the weather or the game last night or about an issue they wanted to discuss. McPherson just seemed to appear and Stewart described how he would suddenly realise that he had company. Ray made some enquiries and a few weeks later McPherson was moved away, no reason was given, he just left. Stewart was beginning to enjoy this new lifestyle and soon began to relax, Alistair was right, it was a good solution. He started to get to know his brother again, they had been separated during their university years, on opposite sides of the country. Driving to meet was out of the question, the journey by road was more than two thousand five hundred miles and flights took six hours, which was not a problem but there never seemed to be time to arrange a get together.

Stewart realised that he had no real need of a big pick up truck for the commute to work and considered that maybe a cycle could be an option. He could ride to the nearest Metro station and it would help him get some exercise to top up his regular swims and gym sessions. He had to admit he was getting used to this life and had even gone shopping to update his wardrobe and now had a collection of smart suits and casual outfits to match his life in the capitol.

He met Marcos from the apartment below, he was from Texas but his surname, Dullum, was from Denmark. His parents had arrived from Denmark about the same time that Albert their father had arrived from Scotland. Marcos owned a property maintenance business that repaired and serviced apartments that were both privately and government owned. He had a fun lifestyle that Stewart admired; he lived in an apartment that was smaller than Alistair's. The apartments were arranged two to a floor except for Alistair's which used the whole top floor, a penthouse. Marcos regularly held dinner parties for twenty or more guests. Very quickly Stewart was invited and while he expected his brother to be there found that Alistair was at other parties, smaller ones, for older guests. He assumed that Alistair was cultivating his interests with influential people. When he looked at the guests at Marcos's parties, he realised he was right, Marcos was a few years younger than he was and his guests were mainly a little younger than that, mostly middle thirties.

One of the guests was younger than that, he estimated she was younger than thirty. She was circulating and sat down near to him.

"Hi, excuse me but you look just like someone I know."

"I only moved here recently from the West Coast."

"I love the Pacific Coast, my names Angelica, by the way, but everybody calls me Angel."

"I'm Stewart."

She was attractive wearing a tight yellow dress, too short which meant she had to be careful when she sat down. She was now facing him, and her thighs had his attention, too much attention so he switched to her bosom. Ample was the only description and they made the problem worse, so he concentrated on her face. The slight smile told him that she knew what he was doing; she leaned forward and spoke quietly. She should not have leaned forward but he was not complaining.

"Very warm in here, are you alright?"

"Perfectly, could not be better." He changed the subject.

"Do you live here?"

She nodded. "Falls Church, its west of here."

"I moved here less than a month ago."

"I'll bet you are CIA, everybody who lives near me is CIA."

Stewart almost laughed; the CIA are supposed to protect their identities, but everybody seems to know where they live. Probably the agents tried a bit harder but the admin staff did not bother, except they knew things that were best not talked about.

"Wrong, I work for Boeing." Stewart was not sure who he really worked for, it was one of the many companies that worked together but Boeing paid his wages so he, in his mind worked for Boeing. He decided not to mention that he was based in a CIA building, it would complicate matters.

"What's your last name?"

"Phillips."

"I work for the FAA, Federal Aviation Authority at the head office, the one near to the Capital and I deal with Boeing all the time and I've never heard of you."

"We have more than one hundred and fifty thousand employees, you won't know them all."

She laughed. "Stupid me. But wait a minute, Phillips are you related to Alistair who lives above?"

"Brother, and I now live with him."

"I knew you looked familiar; you could be his twin. Alistair's a single man, are you single?" Stewart nodded and the subject was closed.

"I've been told that his apartment is something else, will you show it to me, when Alistair's away that is?"

He smiled as he now knew which way the wind was blowing. They drifted apart but as he was leaving, she handed him a small business card.

"Give me a call and we can arrange dinner sometime." He knew she was thinking further ahead than that but said nothing and gave her a peck on the cheek.

Alistair was drinking Scotch when he entered their apartment, so he joined him.

"Good dinner party?"

"Very good, I met somebody who knew you, called herself Angel."

"Ah, Angel what can I say. Be very careful with that one, she eats men like us for breakfast."

"She asked a lot of questions and I got the impression that she already knew the answers."

"She claims to be FAA but I'm not sure."

Neither was Stewart but he did not say so. She was either naturally inquisitive or she collected information for others.

"She is curious about this apartment."

"Don't know why she's been here on a couple of occasions. As I said be careful."

Alistair was implying that he knew of his brother's security standing but he had never discussed it with him.

Chapter Five.

Stewart put the conversations with Alistair and Angel to one side as he had more important things to deal with at work. These involved national security and had to be dealt with and were of such magnitude that both he and Ray had been summoned to a meeting at the White House with the President. Stewart returned to the apartment after that momentous meeting still in a state of shock to find Alistair in the kitchen brewing a pot of coffee. Alastair seemed surprised as Stewart walked in dressed in one of his smart grey suits complete with matching socks and tie, not his usually workday attire.

"Wow, you are looking smart for a working day, have you been somewhere special?!"

Stewart sat down. "You will not believe it when I tell you. I still cannot get my head around it, I have just come from the White House".

Alastair turned round quickly. "You are kidding me? The White House, next you will be telling me you were in the Oval Office".

Stewart laughed, "Well not exactly, Ray, that is my colleague, and I were shown into a very nice conference room for our meeting with the President".

Alastair almost choked on his coffee. "You met the President? I cannot believe it. Was it a big meeting and why were you there?"

"The meeting was just the two of us, the President and his security men, a very private and personal meeting. We were there to explain our work and a problem that has arisen which could have a huge impact in the future. Now if you do not mind, I need to get changed, write up some notes and have some time to think. So I will take a cup of coffee and a donut and bid you goodnight."

Stewart went to his room leaving Alistair with no chance to ask more questions. He was beginning to realise that his brother was just a little bit more than a guy who meddled with computers, he would treat him with a little more respect in future.

A few days later Stewart arrived at the apartment later than usual, Alistair was away in New York, so he picked up an Italian takeaway and was just through the door when his phone rang. It was Angel.

"Hi Stewart, how are you. I'm downstairs at Marcos's place; can I come up and see you?"

He was trying to think of a good reason to say no without hurting her feelings but could not.

"On my way."

He stood still with the takeaway in one hand and his phone in the other; he could hear the elevator ascending. He put the food in the kitchen area and went out onto the landing as the elevator doors opened. She stepped out and looked stunning, she could have dressed like that for a party but not for everyday wear. As with the yellow dress that she wore to the party the red one she was wearing was too short and the off the shoulder style presented him with the same choice that he had had at the party. Legs, thighs, bosom, or face it was an assault on his senses that he had always assumed women did not understand but used effectively. They moved into the apartment and she closed the door with her foot.

"I brought an Italian back with me."

"We don't need him, send him away."

"Italian food."

"We don't need that either."

She pushed him back against the wall and pressed herself close to him and they moved across the room. Out of the corner of his eye he saw Marco's car drive into its parking place and Marco got out, he was carrying two briefcases. Angel kissed him and forced a leg between his.

She was saying something. "I thought with Alistair being away it was too good an opportunity to miss."

A switch closed in Stewarts' head; she had said she was down below at Marco's place, but he had just seen him arrive home, also she had said that Alistair was away. How did she know that; Alistair had left unexpectedly that morning on the early flyer to New York? Alistair had been going out of the door and shouting goodbye while he was still in the shower.

"Must be urgent." He called after him.

Then there was the telephone call, Stewart had taken it on his company phone. How did Angel know the number? She had given him her business card at the dinner party, but he had not given his card to her. Also, if he had it would have been his private card. He knew that there could be a genuine explanation, but he did not think so. Her hand was going down into his slacks and trying to figure it out was not easy, also he was running out of breath.

"Stewart you're not concentrating, you're not with me."

"I'm not, the truth is I'm worn out, had nothing to eat all day and need sleep."

"Let me take you to bed, I'll relax you."

"And I'll fall asleep on you."

She stared at him and made a quick decision; he saw it on her face.

"I've been unfair; we'll put it on hold until the weekend. I am not sure what I was thinking of; I will leave you in peace. Please forgive me."

With that she backed away, smoothed her dress and hair, and made for the door. He escorted her to the elevator and patted her backside as she stepped inside. As the doors closed, he turned quickly and re-entered the apartment, from the window he saw her cross the parking area and walk towards a parked car. The lights had come on as she approached the car and she got into the passenger side; it drove quietly away. He could tell it was a Tesla but due to being five stories above he could not read the number plate. Also, the street lighting was off-white, and he could not be certain of the colour, it was probably red. The Italian had gone cold, so he put it in the microwave, transferred it to a plate and took it to the dining room. He no longer felt tired and ate slowly. How had she known his works number, how had she known that Alistair was away, those two questions were going round and round in his head. She could have got his number from Alistair or from somebody at the FAA office; there were a lot of possibilities. He decided he would speak to Alistair the following night and would have the CIA check her out when he went to work in the morning. He went to bed with the thought that she would have been there with him.

Next day he reported in, as he was duty bound to do so, any unusual security breach. He felt a fool, was she just a bit over friendly; the CIA officer obviously thought the same way and said so.

"So, a very pretty woman visits your apartment, uninvited, and tries to get you into bed and you threw her out. Are you not normal?"

"I was tired."

"Tell me what you know about her."

"I don't even know her last name, she is Angelica and works for the FAA at their head office."

"Right I'll get back to you as quick as I can." The CIA agent was amused.

He was busy all day and forgot about the incident until the agent rang him.

"Agent Spencer Coltrane here sir, further to your call this morning. We have run all the usual checks on Angelica Krasinski, known to you as Angel. She works for the FAA, has done for four years as a secretary, nothing unusual in her employment records. Lives in Falls Church in the family home as Mrs. Chapman, her husband died while on holiday five years ago, before she joined the FAA. She reverted to her maiden name after her husband's death; it usually pays off in some jobs as you tend to stand out. Her father is an Italian and her mother, Mary Hampson, is English. Both parents are alive and are US citizens, they live in Baltimore. We have checked for any known contacts that would be interested in your work and did not find anything, we already had her on a watch list and will keep you informed. You did the right thing checking on her; in your line of work you must be careful. Our advice would be to get her into bed as soon as you can." He rang off.

Alistair was in the apartment when he got home. His trip to New York had been fruitful which made him happy as he had woken during the night and made the decision there and then to go and close off a lucrative deal. He had eaten before leaving New York so Stewart made them a light snack. As he poured some wine Stewart decided to question his brother, he explained the events off the previous night Alistair interrupted.

"Stewart, Stewart you don't have to feel guilty, I had a great time with Angel but she becomes boring, so I moved on. You know, greener grass and all that."

"So, you knew her for a long time?"

"If three months is a long time?"

He had never thought of his brother like that, but he was a single man.

"I did warn you to be careful with that one. Why did you involve the CIA, she's a harmless secretary for goodness sake?"

"I know that now."

"Wait a minute, why did you involve the CIA?"

Stewart hesitated, despite knowing of the meeting at the White House his brother still thought of him as a software programmer.

"Why did you involve the CIA?"

Alistair was leaning across the table, demanding answers.

"Because my job is highly classified."

"What does highly classified mean?"

"I can't tell you."

"What do you mean, you can't tell me. I'm your brother for goodness sake."

"The rules are simple; I don't speak to anybody about my work and that includes family members."

"Is that why you are based at a CIA office building?"

"Partly, I was a security risk when I was working in Seattle but that changed when part of the specialised unit that I worked for moved here. They wanted to be closer to the government offices and the FAA and CIA."

"Does that security extend to this apartment?"

Stewart did not answer."

"Does it?"

"Yes, it does."

"And me and my friends?"

"Probably, I don't have anything to do with security."

He did not say that the reason he reported Angel's activities was because for some reason her actions had worried him. He was an average man and her intense interest bothered him. He now knew he had done the right thing after hearing Alistair's revelations about her. If he had not reported in, they would have been wondering why, especially if they had been watching her and seen her arrive at the apartment when he was alone. But why had they been interested in her and not voiced their concerns during their conversation earlier.

Alistair startled him from his thoughts. "Stewart you have to explain yourself."

Before he could answer his phone rang, it was Agent Coltrane. He moved away from the table as Alistair cleared the plates and was pouring fresh coffee as he sat down.

"That was the agent that I reported into earlier, the one who told me that Angel was not a security risk." He went silent as he gathered his thoughts.

"So why is he contacting you now."

"The man she was married to, Alan Chapman was not Alan Chapman. The real Alan Chapman had disappeared on a hiking holiday."

"But they married?"

"Yes, someone called Alan Chapman came back from the hiking holiday."

"Who was he, what was his name?"

"We don't know anything about him."

"Him, were they watching him or her?"

"Both."

" For five years and the CIA doesn't know anything about them, that's amazing."

"They weren't actually watching them; they were on a watch list as they had no reason to watch them closely but when they appeared here, they were noticed."

"What was it that got their attention?"

"She was training to be an airline pilot when she became ill, she got rheumatic fever. That finished her pilot career, so the airline redeployed her in a training unit where she taught navigation. That made me sit up, I work on navigation systems, top secret navigation systems."

"Have they arrested her?"

"No and they are not going to, my instructions are to get to know her. I will be fully briefed tomorrow."

"Not all bad then, she can be lively in bed."

Alistair was not concerned that his apartment was going to be used for sexual entertainment.

"Yes, but I won't be, with them listening in."

Alistair looked around wildly.

"Are we being recorded?"

"Not yet but we will be, I am instructed to tell you what I do and enlist your help. I think you are going to be away from time to time."

"We got there in the end; I'll make some fresh coffee. How long will this explanation take?"

"Hours."

Chapter Six.

They moved into the living room and settled into comfortable chairs. Stewart sat for a while thinking about how he would explain the last eighteen years of his life. He had never talked to his mother or his father about it and certainly not to any of his friends.

"I can give you the bare information or I can tell you the whole story, which do you prefer?"

"Let's hear the full story."

"Could take hours."

"For goodness sake just get on with it."

"OK, it starts back in the sixties when hi-jacking was popular. A man armed with a handgun would walk into the cockpit and say something like. 'Take me to Cuba', they were escaping from something or other. It was a regular thing; in 1960 for instance there were more than one hundred hi-jacks in the United States alone. "

Alistair was nodding but Stewart knew that his brother did not fully understand, the events that he had mentioned took place years before they were born.

"This became such a problem that the authorities had to do something; their first reaction was to prevent guns getting on aircraft. Passengers were checked before boarding, physically at first, then with X-rays later but by that time the terrorist organisations had realised the potential of hijacking. They devised ways of beating the system, which included making guns out of plastic, and dissembling them so that the individual items were not identifiable by x-rays or by using threatened cabin staff to hide a gun in one of the toilets. Then Sky Marshalls were deployed, they were armed men who appeared to be holiday makers or businessmen and were seated near the front where they could intercept hi-jackers making for the cockpit. When that did not work, and it was not a good idea to have a shootout on an aircraft anyway they decided that if the hi-jacker could not get into the cockpit he could not take control of the plane. Bullet proof doors were fitted to the cockpit and that worked even though the hi-jackers would drag an airhostess to the door and threaten to shoot her unless the door was opened. Bullet proof doors are still fitted to most airliners. The real problem was that a hi-jacked airliner was good publicity for a terrorist organisation. One such hi-jacking involved two airliners owned by a British company that were hi-jacked and landed on a war time emergency landing strip in the Sahara Desert. The terrorists allowed the hostages to walk away and for the television media to get into good filming positions before they blew the cockpits off the aircraft. It was spectacular."

Alistair was taking a keen interest. "I did not realise you were involved with all this stuff."

"I was not, we were still at hi-school." He gave his brother an exasperated glare.

"This is part of the whole story, not just my involvement."

"Got you."

"Then the terrorists came up with their best hi-jack. By sending a small team over here to learn to fly, they went through basic training and graduated onto aircrew training. These trained pilots were employed by the airlines and were destined to become just like the kamikaze pilots of World War Two."

"Who did not care whether they died or not."

"That is exactly right and they died after they flew the hijacked airplanes into the World Trade Centre and the Pentagon, they killed thousands. The events of 9/11 were an awakener for everyone as we had no defence for such acts. By the time anyone realised what was happening it was too late to shoot them down even if we had planes or missiles in place. If they had been shot down then the debris would fall on the city and as the passengers were, mainly, US citizens no one would have liked to make that call."

"Difficult."

"More like impossible, because if they selected targets and airfields that were close together, we wouldn't have time to work out their plan or what was happening. After 9/11 the President, George Bush Jnr made an unguarded comment at a meeting. He said, 'we have got to do something about those folks.' People from the aviation industry who were within hearing range flinched because they knew Boeing and Honeywell were already working on it and expected the President to be informed".

"I'm confused, how were Boeing and Honeywell working on such a high-profile project without the President knowing?"

Stewart sighed, "Because they weren't officially working on it."

"But you just said…"

"I know but it was not quite like that. Boeing and Honeywell had been working for a long time on remote control systems for military aircraft and were looking for a way to recoup some of their investments. I will explain, early missiles were simply like a firework; you lit the fuse paper and stepped back. Hopefully, the missile went to where you had pointed it. The missiles that the Germans launched in World War Two were like that, very hit or miss but effective when they hit the right place. Guidance systems changed that, the current Cruise missiles fly at fifty feet over the sea and one hundred feet over land. They are guided by GPS and are very accurate; you do know what GPS is?"

"Of course, don't get testy with me; I live in a different world than you. A world that generates dollars that pays for these toys."

Stewart ignored the outburst and carried on.

"We now have drones that fly to other countries and take photographs; we have unmanned fighter aircraft and unpiloted transport aircraft. As a way of recouping their investment on military drones Boeing and Honeywell saw unmanned airliners as the way forward. NASA looked like an ally, they had a 747 Jumbo that was equipped, by Boeing Honeywell, for unmanned flight and as a first step they applied to fly it in the airways amongst passenger airliners. Their requests were turned down, despite many attempts mostly because the FAA thought that the idea was not safe, and the flying public would not accept it. Would you get on an airplane that did not have a pilot?"

"I'd have to think about it. If there was an alternative with a pilot, I would choose that one."

"Typical answer."

"So, what happened?"

"The idea was not shelved, and Boeing and Honeywell worked on the program. At one stage Honeywell had five hundred computer programmers working on it. And other systems were catching up, fly by wire was fitted to all airliners and Autoland was also fitted to nearly every model."

"Fly by wire and Autoland, you'll have to explain."

"When aircraft first flew the controls were moved by flexible steel cable that ran over a pulley system, as the aircraft grew larger the controls became too heavy for the pilot so hydraulic assistance was introduced, this was heavier and more complicated. Current aircraft use a new system called 'fly by wire' which uses electrical components to do the work. There are some race cars and motorcycles that use this system and it is being continually improved. Autoland is based on a bombing system from World War Two; it enables the plane to land without the pilot in control which is especially useful in bad weather. This can only be done at suitably equipped airfields. Both these systems can be controlled by the navigation computer installed into the airplane. Adding these enhancements to standard navigation software meant that it was possible for an aircraft to take-off, fly a pre-planned route and land without human intervention. The only problems were the concerns of the FAA and the reluctance of the passengers to accept pilotless aircraft. There is a huge pilot shortage which is making the problem worse, so Boeing set out to demonstrate that everything was in place for the safe operation of a pilotless aircraft. They constructed a dirt strip runway in the Mojave Desert to demonstrate the ability to land and they also flew their Boeing 747 aircraft with pilots in the back, usually playing cards, and nobody up front in the cockpit for hundreds of take offs and landings."

"I had no idea about this, was it ever reported?"

"Was it ever reported, have you been asleep or something?"

"I suppose I am just like the rest of the population; you turn up at the airport and everything just works, you get to your destination without any drama. So, what changed, anything?"

"The Boeing Honeywell Uninterruptable Autopilot known as the BHUAP."

"A long name for a piece of equipment, I'll bet it is all in a little metal box."

"It isn't, it is in two parts which can't be separated electrically, the navigation system and the fly by wire both depend on both parts. Its principle is really simple but ingenious. All airline aircraft have an autopilot and the BHUAP is connected to it, the pilot sets the speed and the height, and the direction is inputted from the autopilots own memory using data supplied by Jeppesen. Once the autopilot is set the pilots in the cockpit can relax as everything is taken care of until they receive instructions for a change of height or direction from an air traffic controller due to weather. Any conflicting traffic is dealt with by the systems and changes would be made automatically using the latest versions of the anti-collision radar."

Stewart paused, he hoped that Alistair was understanding all this and relaxed when Alistair commented that he had no idea that so much of the control of an aircraft was now automatic and the pilots were just needed for take-off and to reassure the passengers.

Stewart smiled and continued. "Well they do a little bit more than that, especially when something goes badly wrong like the recent bird strike after take-off where the pilot took immediate control of the aircraft and landed on the Hudson River. An automatic system would never have been able to make that split second decision, it would have to go through all the known scenarios and by then the aircraft would have crashed. So skilled and well-trained pilots will still be a vital part of the safety of aircraft journeys and it will be some time before they are completely redundant."

Alistair nodded in agreement. "So what exactly are you doing then, working on these automated systems or something completely different?"

"I have been part of the team involved in the development of the BHUAP which can take over the control of an aircraft in the event of a hi-jack or similar situation. If anyone, flight crew or passenger, attempts to interfere with the autopilot settings or if somebody attacks the cabin door the pilot operates a switch, known as the hi-jack button. This sends a signal to the air traffic controllers and a pre-planned operation is automatically set-in motion. Control is immediately transferred to a central controller and the aircraft is flown remotely to the closest safe airfield to land, the pilots are then just passengers. Control of the aircraft to the onboard crew or hi-jackers cannot be restored while the aircraft is airborne and can only be reset by engineers through a control panel on the outside of the aircraft. All the voice communications, including any mobile phone or satellite phone signal, with the aircraft can be disconnected which prevents threats to passengers and crew."

"That's fantastic." Alistair was genuinely amazed. "So, this system is already in use now?"

"Thousands of aircraft have been fitted with the upgrade and this went part of the way to proving the case for unpiloted airliners."

"Why say part of the way, surely it means they are proven?"

"Not quite, the authority's wanted the take-off system tested but Boeing had anticipated this and working with another company, General Atomic, who build military drones, they built large drones to civilian standards. Called Sky Guardian Atomic they were being delivered to many air forces on the other side of the Atlantic. To do this they flew them in civilian airspace which they were entitled to do as they conformed to all civilian regulations. One of the first of these drones was delivered to the Royal Airforce in England and took off from Grand Forks, North Dakota, and navigated US airspace, flew the Atlantic Ocean and entered British airspace before landing at an airfield in Southern England. British airspace is the most complex in the world, especially around Heathrow, London due to the size of the country and all the traffic from the Americas to all the European countries. The Sky Guardian had proved the concept, which was a relief as the BHUAP had already been fitted to tens of thousands of aircraft."

Stewart paused and took a drink before he continued.

"Then came a shock as there were several aircraft that were deliberately crashed by a member of the crew but the BHUAP was not deployed to save them. For example, a Malaysian airliner went missing on a flight from Kuala Lumpur to Beijing and despite the search being the largest in aviation history in time, cost and the number of countries taking part it has not been found. Parts of the aircraft have been found in the Indian Ocean, but the best explanation is that it is five miles under the surface in the Southern Indian Ocean; it has been missing for more than five years."

"I heard about this."

"It is like the biggest aviation mystery of modern times; it will always be there to haunt us."

Alistair had been following the lengthy explanation.

"So now your job is to find the location of that aircraft by tracing the BHUAP that was on board?"

"No, we cannot trace it and if we could it wouldn't be possible to bring it to the surface, five miles depth of water in the world's most dangerous ocean makes that impossible. We will never know the fate of that airliner and the more than two hundred passengers on board."

"So, everybody decided to forget about it?"

"Everybody started asking questions, especially why control of that aircraft was not taken over by the BHUAP early in the flight when it was about to leave Malaysian airspace. At that point it was obvious to a lot of people that something was wrong and that despite the anti-hijack button not being pressed the BHUAP may have been able to save the lives of everybody on board. Someone or a group of people decided not to use it. Since then there have been other cases where the BHUAP should have taken control but it was not used. The question everyone should have been asking is, 'why was it not used?'"

Alistair was thinking hard, it was a lot to take in and understand and as Stewart glanced out of the window, he was surprised to see that the light was fading, it was going dark. He had not realised how long they had been talking. He got up and turned some lights on and as he did, he decided that he had told his brother enough.

"What time is it; we should have something to eat."

"There are some cold meats in the fridge I got them from the deli."

While they were eating and washing it down with California Rose Alistair returned to the discussion.

"Finish what you were saying, you said there were people who wanted to know why that remote control system has never used to save lives."

Stewart had reached a point where he thought it might be prudent to stop talking.

"There are people who were offering all sorts of ideas to explain the disappearance of MH370 from giant flying saucers that scooped it out of the sky to theories that it had landed somewhere."

"That sounds reasonable."

"What have they done with the two hundred passengers, have they kept them prisoner for the last five years. All the theories have been debunked, MH370 is on the seabed in the Indian Ocean and before you ask it is in a thousand pieces and so are the people who were on board. When ships sink, they usually go down in one piece, when aircraft hit the water they break up. Why are we discussing this, I'm not involved in any way with the crashing of any aircraft?"

"So why is your work top secret?"

Stewart groaned. "Why are we discussing this, I agreed to tell you about my work, but I did not agree to analyse it."

"Finish the story."

Stewart sat quietly for a while before agreeing.

"OK but you don't talk to anybody about it."

"I don't intend to discuss anything that you have told me today with anybody, but you can't blame me for wanting to know the full story."

"Right, the BHUAP device was patented and several amendments were added, in all of them it was described as a device for preventing hi-jacking when a pilot could indicate to people on the ground that there was a problem on board. At some point during the development, maybe even at the very beginning, I do not know, the software was upgraded to enable the aircraft to become a weapon. In other words remote control of the aircraft from the ground could be done at any point during any flight without the need for a signal from the cockpit. The patents were not altered, and no FAA notice was issued, and it was not discussed in government circles, but it was changed. It went from a system that could save lives to one that could be used as a threat. A highly effective weapon."

Chapter Seven.

Stewart explained how military power had changed post World War Two. At that time, the USA was definitely in control, as the only country that had nuclear weapons, the only country that had deployed nuclear weapons, we were definitely in control.

"To be fair we prevented the use of nuclear weapons for seventy-five years and it could even be said the risk of major war. Despite our efforts many countries, eight to be exact, produced nuclear devices and our response was to introduce agreements to prevent further proliferation and eventually to reduce numbers."

Alistair seemed to know about this situation but was not sure about the present military situation. Stewart had to explain that a new type of weapon system was becoming commonplace. Originally the missiles were huge and could be launched on any worldwide target; the latest ones were much smaller and shorter range. With satellite surveillance it was impossible for the larger missiles to be fuelled for a first strike without being detected; the later small missiles used solid fuel and were always ready for use. All the capitals of the European countries could be attacked within a noticeably short time without any signs of preparation in a first strike scenario.

Stewart continued, "the BHUAP offered a retaliation that could not be countered, and it is effective, it could not be ignored. Very cleverly the un-alterable autopilots had been introduced into most of the world's airliners under the guise of preventing hi-jacking. Aircraft already airborne can be taken under control and others about to take off could be taken over soon after they left the ground and they would be guided remotely to a suitable target which they would reach in minutes. It meant that any belligerent governments would have to think twice before commencing military activity. The price to pay could involve their key buildings being destroyed. They could only imagine an Airbus A380 weighing five hundred and fifty tons of which eighty tons is fuel coming through the front door of their parliament building. Even if it were smaller aircraft, say five Boeing 727's the result would be devastating. From the US point of view they already had all they needed, there are always a large number of suitably equipped aircraft in the air at any given time and they can be used to destroy any

22

target they wish, government buildings, airports, nuclear power stations, missile sites and even warships. The occupants of all those targets would be killed and the country would become leaderless. It would be difficult to shoot the approaching aircraft down as the debris would fall on the city and the downed aircraft would immediately be replaced by a second wave. There is a moral question regarding the innocent civilians on board, these are numbered in hundreds compared to the eighty-two thousand who were killed by the first nuclear weapon. If a foreign country attacked us now with a modern nuclear weapon which is more powerful than the wartime version, a million people could die."

"In that case it makes sense to disable their country." Alistair had seen the logic in the military argument. He was seeking clarification.

"How many airliners are fitted with these devices?"

"I don't know the exact number but there are more than twenty thousand airliners in use worldwide, and we add another two thousand each year, but as to how many have BHUAP fitted is a different question."

"But if it is only ten percent of them, that's two thousand missiles we can use, that we don't have to provide and service?"

"Yes, but more importantly they are scattered worldwide waiting for us to use them and they can be operational in minutes."

Alistair looked upwards. "I find that scary, all that death and destruction up there and ready for use. I'm glad I'm a US citizen and we are in control."

Stewart did not answer as Alistair was beginning to understand.

"So, what part does Stewart Phillips play in all this, did you design the software?"

There were moments when Stewart thought his brother was special, other times he asked dumb questions.

"I've already told you that at one-point Honeywell had more than five hundred programmers working on the project, so I could hardly design the software myself."

"So what do you do?"

"Hundreds of BHUAP's were already in use when I joined Boeing, were you not listening when I explained all this?"

"So what do you do?" He could become very irritable sometimes.

"When I joined the company, I was working on navigation software and shortly afterwards I joined a guy called Ray Wheeler he was our link to the military. Because of the risk of something happening to him I was his duplicate."

"Before you tell me what he or both of you do it sounds like a good idea."

Stewart had not intended to tell his brother about his actual function but was doing so.

"The BHUAP is controlled from a central computer; in fact, there are two of them at widely different locations. Originally when the system was described as a deterrent to hi-jacking they were in different parts of the world and we knew where they were. Ray and myself trained the operators, I do not need to explain that these were very secure places that were under the control of the CIA. When the military became involved everything changed, the military use different satellites and the software had to be changed so that the CIA operators who would prevent hi-jacking could not access the system that allows the use of airliners as a weapon."

"So did your role change?"

"Yes, it was decided that the department working with the military would relocate to Washington and be based at the same CIA building, when the time was right Ray and I would also move to

Washington. We ceased to be involved in training, the CIA trained their own operators, our role was to work more closely with the military to make all the changes to the software and install the updates. From our offices we are in contact with the people who control the BHUAP devices for military use. We don't know where these control centres are based."

"They will be in the US of course."

"Of course but knowing our military they will be in Las Vegas or a beach resort in California."

"Somewhere highly secure but warm and sunny."

"Exactly, they are connected to the system by satellite links so they can be anywhere. The Brits, the Royal Airforce, use a similar system to control their drones and base the drones on the island of Cypress while the control is from somewhere in England. We designed that remote control system, which is different, the British drones, the anti hi-jacking BHUAP system and our military offensive system are not the same. That is important and I will try to explain".

"I can see where you are heading."

"Two weeks ago, I logged on to the program in order to install an update, routine stuff, and entry was denied. I double checked everything, and Ray joined me, and we were baffled. Clearly someone unknown had entered the system and changed the entry procedure and passwords and we were locked out. We checked the software for the drones and the BHUAP system and they were not affected. Somebody had managed to hack into the military system and has tried to take control of the program that can use the airliners in an offensive manner."

Alistair looked shocked. "They could use it against us. Who was it?"

"No idea we have been trying to find out, without any success. The good news is that they have broken in but can't use the remote-control system."

"I don't understand."

"Breaking into software is the same whatever the application. The initial barrier is the security software and once past that you can access the main application. We can't get past the changed security."

Alistair was not as dumb as he made himself out to be. "When we have problems with the office computers, we reload the software and we are going again."

"We've tried all those things, but they have made some clever changes that we can't reverse until we are inside the program."

"New computer with a fresh version of the software?"

"Tried all that but the only thing that will help is a copy of the new security codes and once we have gained access we insert new procedures so that they can't get back in again."

"How did they learn the entry codes in the first place, if they have somebody who is clever enough to do that then surely, we have a programmer who can do the same for us?"

"Trust me we have some of the best brains in the business and they are struggling. We think that somebody told them what they needed to know".

"How many people knew them?"

"Six, Ray and myself and four top military specialists."

"And they check out?"

"So far."

"Do you think, whoever it is will use it?"

"Hopefully, they can't, they don't know how to."

Stewart could tell Alistair was waiting for him to explain.

"When selecting an aircraft to control the location and the destination and many other variables have to be entered into the program in a certain way. One mistake and the program will shut itself down. They might have already found this out and are trying every alternative. There are thousands and thousands of possibilities, could take months we'll know if they get it right when a strategic target somewhere will be attacked."

"Where can they get that information?"

"From the four people we discussed earlier or from trained CIA operators who work from acronyms."

"But you don't know where the any of the operators are."

"No, and the operators have a personal log in code that they have to enter every time before they press the 'enter' key and that code changes."

"How do the operators know the code has changed?"

Stewart gave his brother an old-fashioned look.

"Stupid me, why would I want to know that."

"I'll tell you because it doesn't matter. The program uses the national lottery results in a way you could not imagine so the code is changed with every new lottery result and as there are fourteen million possibilities it would be impossible to work it out the hard way."

They both went quiet, lost in their own thoughts.

" Stewart, I have one very important question."

"Go ahead."

"How do you think the American people will react to the idea that you will send three hundred, four hundred or possibly five hundred innocent people to their deaths?"

"That's one airplane, we could use more, five or ten."

"Public opinion wouldn't go along with that."

"The alternative is thousands of deaths if a single nuclear strike takes place and there are thousands of nuclear weapons. You are missing the point; we want to deter the use of nuclear weapons. We think, not just the American people, but worldwide the population will realise what is happening."

"I hope you are right."

"I have lived with this for a long time and believe it is the answer."

"Stewart you do realise the danger you are in; you are one of the best chances that they have of finding what they need. Are the CIA and the military taking your safety seriously?"

"I hope so, I seriously hope so."

Alistair stood up and stretched," My head is spinning with all this information. I think we should go to bed and in the morning, I may need you to clarify a few things."

Chapter Eight.

Breakfast for Stewart was usually taken 'on the go' as he travelled to his office while for Alistair it was a more leisurely meal as his commute was a short ride down on the elevator. Stewart walked into the kitchen and the aroma of fresh coffee filled the air, there was also the sound of bacon sizzling in the pan.

Alistair greeted him. "I slept quite well considering our talk last night and decided to make us a cooked breakfast of scrambled eggs, bacon and toast. Will that suit you?"

"Wonderful, I am hungry and I'll get the plates and cups".

The brothers sat down together and Stewart opened the conversation.

"Did you understand most of what I told you last night?"

Alistair nodded, "Mostly but I am not clear about the different systems."

Stewart was not surprised to hear him sounding confused it was a complicated business.

"Let me explain. It could be said that all this drone business started with model airplanes more than seventy years ago."

"It's not new then."

"I'm willing to bet that somebody will say it is older than that, possibly pre-World War Two. You may remember that as kids we played around with radio-controlled airplanes."

"You did, I found girls more interesting."

Stewart stood up and glanced out of the window and saw a man walking from the parking area towards their building.

"Stay away from the windows, we have a visitor."

He dashed into his bedroom and returned with his pistol, checking it was loaded as he re-joined his brother. As he did so the door chime sounded, and the security screen lit up and Agent Coltrane's face came into view. He pressed the speaker button.

"Agent Coltrane how nice to see you."

"Agent Phillips I need to talk to you."

He pressed the lock release button and let him into the building. Alistair who was standing close behind him spoke.

"So its Agent Phillips, you work for the CIA, not Boeing."

Stewart did not answer as he considered he still worked for Boeing. As he heard the elevator stop he un-fastened the door and stepped back, Agent Coltrane gently pushed the door wider with his foot and stepped in and faced Stewart whose pistol was covering him. He did not show any surprise.

"I'm glad to see that you are taking this seriously, I was not sure if I should meet you with my pistol in my hand, I had no way of knowing who was here with you".

Stewart's pistol was covering him and did not waver "I was waiting to see how many people you had with you."

"Just me up here. Please put your weapon away. May I come inside?"

Stewart showed Coltrane into the dining room and introduced him to Alistair.

He refused the offer of coffee. "I have eight soldiers around the building, they are checking out all the premises, business and residential, and all the cars. There is a red Tesla in the car park."

"Has something happened?"

"I am sorry to have to tell you that Ray Wheeler was killed two hours ago on his way to work. Two men tried to take him hostage and Ray pulled a weapon and some shots were fired. One of the men was killed and the other wounded and is in hospital, it does not look good for him but sadly Ray was killed. Both Ray and the wounded man were shot with Ray's gun; it looks like neither of the two kidnappers was armed."

Stewart was trying to keep his composure.

"Where did this take place?"

"Outside a Nando's. Witnesses said a car pulled up and two men got out of the back and tried to force Ray into the car. The police were on the scene very quickly."

"What happened to the driver?"

"He drove away, but there may have been others in the car which is the reason that I considered arriving here with my weapon drawn."

Stewart was visibly shaking, and Alistair put his hand on his shoulder as Agent Coltrane's radio bleeped, it was one of the soldiers.

Coltrane listened for a minute before answering. "Bring her up."

"There's a woman in the apartment below, apparently she arrived in the Tesla. From the description she would appear to be the woman you know as Angel that you told me about earlier."

Angel looked a little dishevelled but maintained her confident attitude.

"Alistair what is going on here, I arrived at Marco's apartment and found he was not at home then these idiots grabbed me. I don't know why."

Coltrane took over. "Was Marco expecting you?"

"No I was surprising him."

"How did you get in?" Angel glared at him.

"I have my own key." One of the soldiers was searching her bag which she clearly was not happy with but did not say anything, he held up two cell phones which he passed to Coltrane who pocketed them. He was not taking any chances.

"Take her in; we'll deal with her later." Angel rounded on him.

"What are you taking me in for? I've done nothing wrong."

"You are a known associate of Alan Chapman."

"Alan, I was married to him for goodness sake, he was my husband."

"That will do for now." She grabbed her bag off the soldier who had searched it and Coltrane took it off her and handed it back to the soldier. The two of them had reached the elevator as Coltrane's radio bleeped.

"I'm on my way down, I'll talk to him." He did not elaborate.

"Please wait here, I'll be back up shortly."

The instruction was for the brothers and the remaining soldier. He was back within ten minutes.

"Marco did not know about her visit or that she had a key, we've taken him in."

Neither Alistair nor Stewart understood what was happening.

"Where have you taken them?"

"To one of our offices, we need to talk to them and yourself. You both need to come with me but I'm leaving some of the soldiers here."

When they got outside, they saw that two heavy trucks were on one of the lawns and the soldiers were settling in.

"How long will they be here?"

"No idea, until you are safe."

Chapter Nine.

Stewart had assumed that they would use Army vehicles, but they were taken to an office building in saloon cars. There were no signs on the building, and they drove through the gates and parked around the back.

"What is this place?"

"You don't need to know."

They were taken to a meeting room which was furnished with a long table and eight chairs; there were two men already there. Clearly, they had been there for some time judging from the coffee cups and papers scattered on the table. It occurred to Stewart that the meeting had not been about the death of Ray; it had been in progress for some time. Spencer Coltrane introduced the two men as Alan Mercer and Martin Steadman, judging from the way he spoke to them they were clearly senior agents who worked closely with him. Coltrane indicated that they should sit and he took a seat near the end of the table and began to speak.

"We have a lot to get through, so I'll start with a quick review of what we definitely know, please shout out if I get anything wrong. We the United States have a software system which can take control of airliners in flight, it can take control of the aircraft and once engaged cannot be disconnected until the aircraft is on the ground. It was conceived to deter hi-jacks and prevent the sort of situation which confronted us at 9/11. Many, no, most airliners are equipped with this system that means whoever owns them or whichever country they are from has not got ultimate control. Despite being designed to deter hi-jacking it was realised, at some disputable point, that this would make an excellent weapon. For that reason and to keep its existence as quiet as possible it has never been used to thwart a hi-jack, even though there have been instances where it would have helped. It was too valuable to expose to it to public scrutiny."

Stewart could see a hand waving. "Does that mean foreign governments are not aware of its existence?"

"Of course they are, and we want them to know, it makes them behave like good boys. The larger countries clearly know that they must be careful, or else. The smaller countries, like Iran or North Korea are frightened to break wind and that is good because they are the countries that could start something that could lead to a bigger conflict. Now I know that you already understand what I have just said but I want it clear in your mind, so I thought early discussion now would prevent any misunderstandings."

Stewart realised that the whole conversation was for the benefit of the two agents who were already in the room when they arrived. Coltrane and himself fully understood the situation but Alistair was an unknown quantity to them, in fact he wondered why he was there.

Coltrane nodded towards Alistair.

"You may not know this gentleman, Alistair Phillips; he is the twin brother of the man sitting next to him, Stewart Phillips who is a computer specialist who works on the software that is used on this new weapon. Stewart worked closely with Ray Wheeler while Alistair is not part of our security system but will be playing an important role in future."

Alistair gave Stewart a questioning look.

"Until recently Alistair was not even aware of the sort of work that his brother was involved with. That is until Stewart gave him a full explanation yesterday."

Alistair's questioning look was replaced by one of puzzlement. Coltrane continued.

"Before either of you ask, the apartment was bugged and you, Stewart did a good job, we are certain it would have taken longer if we had tried to brief Alistair."

"Wait a minute; you can't just bug my apartment without my agreeing." Alistair was protesting.

Coltrane smiled. "We can and we did."

He carried on without taking much notice of Alistair's feelings. Stewart's thoughts were slightly different; he had suspicions about the bugging but had expected Alistair to be a bit more indignant. He realised that Alistair thought it was exciting; he was revelling in the idea that he was doing something for his country. There were a few minutes of silence and Coltrane carried on as though nothing had happened.

"Things have changed, somebody has broken into the system and we have lost control of it."

They were all looking around wildly with expressions of disbelieve.

"Does that mean it could be used against us?" Mercer asked.

Coltrane pointed upwards towards the sound of a departing jet airliner.

"That aircraft could be on its way to the White House right now."

Mercer stood up as though he thought they could stop it. Coltrane told him to sit down.

"I am giving you an example. That aircraft has just left Ronald Regan Airport which is a couple of miles from the White House. If whoever now has control of the system that I explained to you has decided to take control now when it reached two thousand feet, it will make a right turn and line up on the While House. The aircraft would arrive there about two minutes after take-off. On the ground no one is aware of anything but several thousand people over near the White House have only a minute to live. Worse still there could be other aircraft following behind this one."

For a moment there was silence. Steadman spoke "How do we stop it?"

"We can't, there is no defence against this system, we built it well, except."

"Except what?" Steadman was now shouting at Coltrane.

"When they broke into the software, they only got past the first security checks but can't use the actual software. There are only a few people who understand that. They somehow managed to get past the security check and changed the password and other checks so that we can't use it."

"We are locked out?" Coltrane nodded. "They have got into the program but can't use it, we can't get access but if we did, we could use it?"

Mercer was up on his feet again.

"So it is a race, we have to regain control and they have to find out how to use it. We will know the winner when they find they can no longer control the program and we will know they have succeeded when the White House or similar disappears. We all saw the devastation when the World Trade Centre was attacked."

Stewart had been sitting quietly. "They might gain access and not use it; we would never know that they had succeeded but they would have total control. We are talking here about Washington, but it could be any city in the world and any target. It depends on who they are, at the moment we have no idea."

Coltrane pointed to them all in turn. "I think a break is in order, would we all like coffee?"

Stewart sat there with his coffee listening to their theories. They only knew the bare facts and it would take hours to explain everything and then they would realise that they were powerless. It was a good decision to take a break, he watched them calm down and when they were sitting quietly Coltrane continued.

Chapter Ten.

"We know the size of the problem, but we don't know who is behind it and how much time we have but we have a plan." Coltrane looked at Stewart for support.

"Stewart, how many people are able to operate this system?"

"Fewer than you would expect, let me explain, the system originated from an earlier system for controlling drones, they are military un-manned aircraft. We developed the system for preventing hi-jacking and that had its own control system, which was operated by a government body, probably the CIA."

He glanced at Coltrane who did not acknowledge what he had said.

"The system for taking control of airliners as a weapon was derived from the previous two and was deliberately different for obvious reasons to avoid the situation we now find ourselves in."

He explained how the software had been modified so that even people who had worked with the previous systems could not operate the new version.

"For the drone software we trained air force and army operators and they ran training schools, for the anti hi-jacking software we did the same thing but with civilian operators. Which means we do not know how many were trained afterwards, or who they are but one thing is certain none of them can help whoever has this software. With the software that we are discussing we only trained four operators, that is two for each of the control points that were scheduled to be set up. These were military personnel and we do not know who they are, where they are based or whether two control points were actually set up."

"What a mess." Mercer muttered but Coltrane corrected them.

"It was intended that way and it worked; they can't operate the system."

"So there are four people out there who can show them how it's controlled, just four?"

Stewart spoke quietly, "No there were two more, Ray Wheeler and I are part of the team of programmers at Boeing, we are the original source."

There was a flurry of movement as everybody in the room realised what he had said.

"But Ray Wheeler has just been killed."

Stewart nodded.

"You are incredibly valuable to these people."

Coltrane raised his hand for silence.

"If we can identify who they are and how they managed to get into the programme, we can take back control and put further security into the software and our problems could be over. We have to protect Stewart and identify the other four people and protect them."

"You said they were probably military, but you don't know, won't that be difficult?"

"Yes and I can't say any more at this stage."

"Have you no idea who is behind this?"

"We can go through all the likely suspects but still miss the right one."

"So who is top of the list, I for one would like to know."

It was Mercer who had spoken, he seemed to want answers; he was probably very senior in the CIA and was smarting because of his lack of knowledge.

Coltrane knew when he was cornered.

"Obviously, Russia and China would like to acquire it; they have large stockpiles of nuclear weapons and don't want that advantage taken from them. But we do not think it is either of them; they would handle this situation in a different way. Russia would release information that would be damaging to us, telling the world how evil we are, China would release information about a new system they have developed. We would know exactly what they are doing but the public would see us in a bad way. After those two we have some nuclear armed countries such as the United Kingdom, France, Israel, India and Pakistan who would think carefully about coming into conflict with the USA."

Mercer was straight in. "They wouldn't be in conflict; they would be in control."

"Being in control with nuclear weapons isn't risk free; any nuclear war would decimate them as well. We do not think it is any of them. The dangerous ones are those who just about have nuclear capability and having control of this system would enhance their standing."

"Which are they?"

"North Korea and Iran, although there could be others that we are not aware of yet."

Mercer was now on familiar ground.

"An unreliable bunch of idiots, they are dangerous. They could start something that they cannot finish. Do you think it is them?"

"Could be but there is another group that we have to consider. If a terrorist group got hold of it, we would be in real trouble."

"Real trouble? We are in real trouble now, but you are right, they would simply want to rule the world and we could not strike back; they do not have a country. I hope it's not them."

Mercer had stated what they all felt.

Coltrane summed up the situation. "We have to identify who it is and recover control of the software. That is absolute priority."

Steadman had been listening but not saying much.

"You said you had a plan, let's hear it."

Chapter Eleven.

There was a knock on the door and Coltrane's secretary entered clutching some notes and two mobile telephones. She apologised for the interruption.

"Two phones Sir, taken from Mrs. Chapman. One is new or rather has not been used, no contacts and no messages. It is registered in the name of Angelica Krasinski. The other is registered in the name of Alan Chapman and has many contacts listed and lots of data and telephone contacts. None of them seem to be of interest but we are still checking. Her car, a Tesla is registered in the name of Angelica Chapman and checks out. The address at Falls Church is the same, no problems there."

"She's squeaky clean, too clean, give her the phones and the car and thank her for her help, release her. We'll keep an eye on her."

The secretary left and Coltrane looked at them all, took a deep breath and explained.

"In order to find the cause of our problem we have to give the perpetrators what they want. They need a programmer or an operator who can help them operate the software that they have taken control of. We have to give them such a person who sadly has to be Stewart here."

He indicated Stewart with a wave of his hand, there was a deathly silence followed by,

"What." It was Mercer who was shaking his head.

"We can't do that, if they get the information out of him, they will have what they want and we will be in danger, all the world could be in danger."

Stewart who was looking bewildered could only say. "You seem to be forgetting me."

"You will be completely safe; they will not harm you because they need you."

"Until they have what they want."

"That's a point but not the important one; we would be giving them total control of the software."

Coltrane held his hand up. "I said we need to give them Stewart but should have said Alistair."

There was complete silence and you could almost hear their brains working. Coltrane explained for those that had not worked it out for themselves.

"They are twins but not totally identical twins; bit if you do not look too closely you can easily mistake one for the other."

Everybody stared at Alistair and Stewart and slowly nodded their heads. Coltrane carried on quickly preventing discussion.

"Fortunately, Stewart explained to Alistair about the software and our problem, so he has a basic understanding. As far as I can find out Alistair has no computer programming knowledge, like all of us he uses and understands computers. He cannot tell them any answers to their problems."

"They'll rumble him and get rid of him; we can't expose him to that."

"He has to identify them, send that information to us and escape."

Stewart had heard enough. "I can't believe you are talking about my brother as though he is expendable."

Mercer and Steadman were shaking their heads with disbelief.

"He isn't trained for this type of operation, he's not a special agent or anything like that, he won't have any support. There has to be another way."

"There probably is but it will take time to set up and we don't have time."

They had reached an impasse so they broke for lunch which would allow them to think about it. Coltrane picked up the phone and spoke briefly and catering staff with trolleys entered the room. Stewart was thinking that Coltrane has got this organised so well he is confident that if we have a short lunch break, we will agree. He moved away with Alistair to a corner where they could talk without the others listening.

"Arrogant bastard, who does he think he is?"

Alistair responded." Actually he's right; it is the only way forward."

"That doesn't mean he can send you into a situation like that, no way."

"I'll do it."

"Are you crazy, I won't let you?"

"Calm down, I said I will do it and I mean it."

They lapsed into silence; Stewart could tell that Alistair had made up his mind.

The trolleys were taken away and Coltrane began to speak but Alistair interrupted him.

"I've thought about what we said and I'm willing to do what you ask. It is the only way available to us, the alternatives risk thousands of lives. I don't want to risk my life and I am sure Agent Coltrane doesn't either."

Mercer wanted more information from Coltrane.

"When did you arrive at this crazy solution?"

"Two days ago when I first saw them together, following that I did a bit of research and it all fitted together. The stumbling block was that Alistair did not understand the software, not the actual software but what it does. Then I heard Stewart to explaining it to him, and he seemed to have a basic grasp of the situation."

"Have you put together a plan for achieving this?"

"Not difficult, we allow them to kidnap Alistair from the apartment. I have made the first steps by placing a guard on the apartment which should tell the perpetrators that Stewart is there, and his safety is a priority. Stewart will assume Alistair's identity and be away on business."

Mercer and Steadman were not in total agreement and wanted Coltrane to make sure that Alistair would be monitored and the discussion and the outcome to be noted and on record. Coltrane agreed and along with Mercer and Steadman escorted Alistair and Stewart down to the garage and they drove away.

When they got back to the apartment block the army had set up a camp on one of the lawns and had erected guard posts at strategic points around the 'gated' community.

Stewart was sceptical. "They'll never get in here."

"There is a way, we have to make it difficult or they might get the idea that something is wrong. Also how they achieve the kidnapping might give us some clues as to who they are. For example, the 'gate' guards or even the soldiers might be involved."

"Surely you don't think that?"

"No, but we have to suspect anybody and everybody. There are for example three apartments below the Phillips apartment, there is the staff at Phillips Investments offices and there are gardeners and maintenance men. A lot of people could be involved."

"I doubt if any Americans would sign up for something like this."

"They will if their families are threatened. But you are forgetting one thing, we want them to succeed, we are not trying to stop them."

"Do the soldiers know that we will be swapping Alistair for Stewart?"

"Definitely not. The only people who know were in that room but that is set to change very shortly, you two, he indicated Mercer and Steadman, and myself have a meeting to attend at the White House. We have to explain ourselves to the President and the head of the National Security Agency (NSA)."

"Are they fully aware of the ongoing situation?"

"Of course, they are waiting for us to sort it out, I report to them regularly."

Chapter Twelve.

Coltrane, Mercer, and Steadman had a brief meeting in the living room while Alistair and Stewart discussed the situation in the dining room. They were well apart so they could talk openly.

"Are you sure you are happy with this?"

"I'd prefer not to be doing it, but I can't think of another way."

"My concern is that you will be dealing with ruthless people, there is a lot at stake for them, and you could be expendable."

Stewart could feel his heart pounding and he was not putting himself at risk, he could only guess how Alistair was feeling.

Coltrane came into the room and he pointed at Alistair.

"Go down to your office and collect some of your papers, cancel any appointments in your dairy and tell your secretary that you are away for a few days break and not to call you, you don't need to explain. Then return here."

Alistair left and returned a short time later carrying his briefcase and reported that his secretary and PA would be dealing with any outstanding matters while he was on vacation. They were not happy about the military presence, but Alistair had explained that it related to a low level threat and was just precautionary and that they should carry on as normal.

"Stewart, you have to change into Alistair's clothes and after the Phillips Investments offices have closed for the day go downstairs and drive away in Alistair's car."

"Where do you want me to go?"

"A taxi will collect you and take you to a secure safe house so you can continue your work but will not need to travel to and from the office. No phone calls or messages just take the time to do more work on the problem."

Pointing at Alistair, "Move into Stewart's bedroom and change into some of his clothes. Do not go into your office, you will be Stewart." He looked a bit grumpy. "I understand."

"Then do exactly what Stewart would do each day. Get up, go to work, return here each night and go to bed."

"Does that mean I have to go on his bike? Can I get another small car or use his pickup? Where do I go to work?"

"CIA building where Stewart works, do not go to his office come up to mine, it is in the same building."

"What do I do all day?"

"To start with you can try to explain to me how this plane thing works. More importantly you will be in my office or out with me. The opposition will see this and assume I am keeping watch over you."

"Do you think they will try and snatch me here?"

"They might."

"How long will this go on for?"

"A long time."

He was wrong. Two days later they were leaving a police station and crossing the road to their car when another car screeched to a halt in front of them and two men leapt out. Coltrane moved to block them and was struck down by a club, despite being injured he clung to his assailant; the other man grabbed Alistair and tried to force him into the back of the car. At that moment two police officers came down the steps from the police station and started running over to help. The two assailants got back in the car; the driver never got out. The car sped off leaving Alistair and Coltrane on the ground, Coltrane was dazed and was helped into the police station where the officers started asking questions. Coltrane showed his CIA identity card and one of the officers that had come to their aid asked,

"What were they after?"

"No idea."

"It's strange; I recognised one of the men. Robbing CIA agents is a step up for him, he is more the 'robbing old ladies' type."

"Do you know where he lives?" The officer was nodding.

"Pick him up and bring him over to my office." He handed over a card and they walked back to Coltrane's car; Alistair decided to drive as Coltrane was angry and cursing.

"Pity about that, if those two officers had not appeared, they would have got you into that car."

"I was doing everything I could without actually helping."

Back at the office Coltrane dropped him by the pickup truck.

"See you in the morning."

Alistair headed for an Italian restaurant hoping he would finish his meal before they tried to kidnap him again.

Chapter Thirteen.

Colorado

At thirty-five thousand feet above Colorado a United Airlines Boeing 740 was cruising at 540 knots, it was a routine flight. Captain Richard (Dick) Harker and First Officer Lewis (Lew) Hillier-Rees had flown the route many times before. The Chicago to Las Vegas run was a prize, they had flown out to Las Vegas the day before and were now making the return journey. The attraction of course was the overnight stop in the fun capital of the world. Dick was into gambling and enjoyed that scene, he was forty-two years old and happily married. One night away from his family was enough and he was heading back, he never got involved with the cabin staff, unlike the majority of captains. Lew on the other hand was twenty-eight and was not interested in gambling, the night life was a break from the routine. The bonus was the endless stream of willing girls that flew into Vegas every day. Many who after finding out he was a pilot declared their undying love for him, but Dick was not interested in anything like that.

On the return leg Dick was always interested in Lew's exploits.

"Tell me about the Russian girl she sounds interesting, you've hooked up with her before?"

"No way, I don't do that, it was another Russian girl that you are thinking about."

"What's wrong with American girls?"

"Absolutely nothing, I judge them all on merit."

Dick was studying the navigation display and he suddenly lost interest in the conversation.

"Have you altered our heading?"

Lew quickly checked his display.

"I see what you mean, we are eight degrees off course."

"Never happened before."

Dick made a decision, he had to, or they would not be going to Chicago.

"Disconnect the autopilot and bring us back to the original heading."

Lew reached for the autopilot controls.

"The autopilot is off."

"Reset the heading and switch it on, pass me the manual."

He wanted the aircraft operating manual to check for known problems.

"It won't switch on."

"Try again."

"Nothing, it's dead."

As experienced pilots they understood the situation, they would have to fly the aircraft manually and navigate. It was not something that they would choose to do but they had been trained for just this situation.

"Amazing, the autopilot develops a fault and the aircraft flies on with only a small change in direction."

"Good old Boeing."

"Call air traffic control and advise them of the situation, we will need their help during the later stages of the flight."

Lew did as he was instructed but quickly reported back.

"They don't answer."

Dick checked with his headset.

"Comms are out, I'll try to find any navigation beacon to check for the signal."

While he was doing that Lew began to check every function in the cockpit and reported that the engines were running as normal, fuel was good, everything looked OK.

"Everything appears to be working except the autopilot, the transponder and the communications equipment, all are turned off and I can't switch them on again."

Dick was thinking hard; they were flying straight and level at the allotted height but on the wrong heading.

"Without the transponder air traffic control may not know where we are, especially after our change of direction."

Lew saw his captain had a puzzled expression on his face. He was mentally checking through all the possibilities.

"Right, the problem is that we have no control over this aircraft. I think that we may have been remotely hijacked."

To illustrate his point he moved the control column and it had no impact on the aircraft. Lew reached for his jacket and fumbled in one of the pockets to find his mobile phone.

Dick commented that it may be off as well.

"It's working." said Lew reaching for the navigation manual to find the entry for O'Hare airport and was relieved to see the telephone numbers of the various departments listed. After several attempts Lew was able to connect with air traffic control and handed the phone over to Dick who set about explaining what was happening. At that point, the internal phone rang, it was Abi Cooke, the senior flight attendant.

"Lew look out of your window, we have a jet fighter slightly behind us, in fact there are two, one on each side. We are having trouble keeping the passengers calm, can you let us know what is happening please? They are taking photographs on their phones and calling their relatives."

Lew looked out of his cockpit window and as he turned back saw that Dick was checking on his side.

"F18 fighters, what's happening?"

Dick described the situation to air traffic control who seemed very calm.

"When you stopped communicating with us and your transponder trace disappeared from our screens, those fighters were scrambled in an attempt to find you."

The controller on the ground had been aware of their problem before they had noticed the change, Dick resolved to be more attentive when in control in future. It was a relief to hear that someone had been alert and that they were doing something.

"What use will they be?"

"It's a precaution, you appear to have changed course and could be on the way to Washington DC."

He handed the phone back to Lew.

"So we are going to Washington DC if I remember correctly this aircraft can now land itself. I hope it works."

Abi was back on the internal phone.

"Captain, the passengers have hooked up to social media who are reporting this as a hijack and showing pictures from Washington where the people are beginning to panic."

Dick realised that the fighter jets were there to shoot them down before the aircraft could impact on a strategic building. They could hear crying and screaming from the passenger cabin but decided against opening the cockpit door.

Lew was shaking, it was all new to them.

"What do you think will happen Dick?"

"It depends on who has hijacked us and why, a good result will be one where we land and walk away. A bad result would be if we flew into a building, deliberately."

Dick picked up the internal phone.

"I have to advise Abi; she has to calm the passengers."

It took him several attempts to locate her, she was in the rear galley.

"Abi listen carefully I am going to tell you what is happening, and you and the other attendants are to advise the passengers. Do not do so by using the address system, move quietly amongst them and explain. Do you understand what I am saying?"

"Yes Captain."

"We have been electronically hijacked, and this flight looks like it is heading for Washington DC. We will be airborne for longer than expected as Washington is further away. We do not know why we have been diverted, but the jet fighters are a precaution and not something to be worried about. Put on the seat belt sign and try to keep the passengers in their allotted seats. Do not elaborate. Have you got that?"

"Yes Captain."

He hung up and exhaled, Lew was watching him but did not speak. They both understood the outcome might not be pleasant. They lapsed into silence.

Chapter Fourteen.

When Alistair arrived at the office next morning, he settled down for a few hours work. Then he went to see Coltrane, who was on the phone and waved him in and pointed to a chair. He was having a very agitated conversation which ended and he put the phone down slowly.

"What was all that about?"

"There is an airliner that has broken off all communications."

"Could this be a hi-jack, usual stuff, somebody on board has taken control."

"That is what air traffic control thought at first, but now they can't talk to the crew."

Alistair moved his chair nearer to the desk.

"Tell me all you know."

"The plane took off from Las Vegas at 7.30am on a routine flight to Chicago; there are two hundred and twenty passengers and crew on board. All was just as normal until after about an hour and a half into the flight when air traffic control received a message from the aircraft to indicate that there was a problem on board. They have a procedure to follow and all was going to plan until they realised that the crew were not communicating with them in the normal way and shortly after that the aircraft position indicator disappeared off their screens. The aircraft appeared to make a turn but they are not sure where it is heading. The person controlling the plane is not following the usual emergency procedure".

"What is a position indicator?"

"Apparently it's a device called a transponder. I have just had it explained to me. On the air traffic control radar the aircraft appears as a 'blip' and next to that 'blip' the transponder displays some numbers that indicate which aircraft it belongs to. Otherwise the screen would be covered by blips and the controller wouldn't know which aircraft was which."

Alistair asked "So, the blip is vital?"

"The blip will still be there but without any information beside it."

"You look worried."

"I am worried, at first they were able to talk to the co-pilot on his cell phone but that has been disconnected. So what we have is an airliner blundering through the sky and air traffic control must try to keep other traffic separated from it. It's an aerial collision about to happen."

"Could it be that someone has found a way to use the new military software?"

"From what Stewart told us that isn't possible. They would need Stewart or one of the other four operators. We do not know where those operators are, could they have found them?"

"I'll find out." Coltrane picked up his phone and started talking; it was a short call.

"They will call me back, they asked me to check if you were still here, I told them that Stewart was seated in front of me."

"It has to be one of the other operators."

His phone rang, it was the FAA who advised him that two fighter jets had been scrambled by the air force to look for the airliner. They were in the air within ten minutes of contact being lost.

"It sounds like they had already put something in place to guard against an occurrence like this." Coltrane nodded and continued.

"The next step for them is when they find it, do they follow it or shoot it down? That depends on where it is heading and where it is. If it is over open countryside the debris will still hurt some people as against over a city where thousands could be affected."

The phone rang again, it was air traffic control to say that the airliner had been located and the fighter pilots had identified it by the number on its fuselage. When they flew as close as possible, they saw people were waving at the windows. One of the crew in the cockpit was trying to tell them something by sign language but they could not understand. It was probably the captain who was shaking his head and holding his hands in the air, he was probably telling them that he was no longer in control. The aircraft was not in the airway to Chicago; it was headed for Washington DC, but it could be headed to any place along that airway.

Coltrane contacted the leader of a specialist team of people who were prepared for just this type of situation and would begin to check the crew and passengers for any known connection to a terrorist or extreme group. His phone rang again; air traffic control was advising him that they had cleared the airway around the airliner to reduce the risk of a collision and it was still looking like Washington DC was the chosen destination. Coltrane asked if that meant an airport at Washington or the White House. Air traffic control told him that they had no way of knowing and that it could still change direction. Coltrane realised that the situation was out of their control, if the airliner overflew the airport and headed directly to a government target, there would only be a couple of minutes to decide whether to destroy it. At that moment, the airliner would be directly over the city. Coltrane was now very concerned. "We need to talk to your brother."

"You don't know where he is."

"He has a satellite phone which is more secure than a cell phone, but I don't want to call him if I can avoid it."

The television news channel had got hold of the story of the hi-jacked airplane from all the social media streamed out by the passengers on board before communication was lost and they watched as preparations were made to receive it at either Ronald Regan Airport or Dulles Airport. The story was blown up out of all proportion; terminal staff were interviewed who explained that all the passengers who were expecting to land at Chicago would need ongoing flights. Security chiefs explained how they would handle the hi-jacker and how they would contain the aircraft when it landed. A veteran security agent related how in the 1960's there had been hundreds of hi-jackings every year.

"They are in for a shock when they find out there isn't a hi-jacker on board, they won't even be able to interview the pilot about what the hi-jacker said or wanted."

Alistair had said what was Coltrane's worst fear. He knew that anytime soon the public, worldwide, would know the worst. He could not imagine the outcry from foreign governments.

When the satellite phone on his desk rang, Coltrane was delighted to hear Stewarts voice he remembered to address him by the correct name.

"Hi Alistair, how are you?"

"I'm fine."

"Lucky you, we have a bit of a problem here. Stewart's working on it."

He knew Stewart would realise he was talking about his brother Alistair.

"I've just seen the television news it would appear to be a hi-jack."

"They seem to have found a way to persuade someone to use the system. If they have, our plan to identify them will not work so you could return."

"Don't be hasty, has any attempt been made to take me hostage?"

"They tried a kidnap with a car, but it did not work."

"In that case stay with the original plan."

"Explain."

"Well, it's only my thoughts, so don't hold me to it but I think the high-jack button must have been used in the cockpit, one of the pilots has been persuaded to co-operate and they have also found one of the CIA control centres which means they have access to two operators. They have persuaded one of them to do a simple run with a hi-jacked aircraft. "

"How would they persuade him?"

"With money or threats to his family. All he would have to do is take control of an aircraft and land it safely. Nobody gets hurt but the landing will be at a sensitive location."

"Washington D.C."

"That would do, because we wouldn't know if it was going to an airfield or somewhere else. Where is it now?"

"Not far from Washington."

" They are teaching us a lesson. If this is what is happening, they still need me because the CIA operators can use the anti hi-jack software but cannot sort any problems with it, they need me. The CIA guys would call Ray or myself if they had a problem. We knew them by first name but not where they were based."

A thought occurred to Coltrane that if Stewart were kidnapped the kidnappers would have to keep him for a long time, for as long as they wanted to use the software, possibly for years.

Alistair (Stewart) rang off with the words.

"Leave everything as it is."

As Coltrane put his satellite phone down his cell phone rang, it was air traffic control to inform him that the hi-jacked airliner had landed at Ronald Regan Airport but had stopped on the runway. The passengers and crew had disembarked which was a hazardous operation with the engines running, but the aircraft still had the runway blocked and was stationary. This was causing a severe backlog at the airport as no other aircraft could land or take off. The ground crew did not want to tow the aircraft with the engines running while they did not have control of them and decided that the best cause of action was to turn off the unalterable autopilot which could only be done from the outside of the aircraft. They expected the airfield to be out of service for at least one hour.

Coltrane was looking for answers so he called Stewart again.

"Are you certain that those operators can only use the anti-hijack software and are not able to use the remote military software. Because there is no other explanation for what has just happened."

"There is and I told you what has probably happened."

"Simple, somebody on that aircraft pressed the 'hijack' button. As there were only two people in that cockpit it must have been the captain or the first officer. Ask the CIA at the airport to detain the captain and first officer, all the cabin crew and passengers. Tell them to make sure that the aircraft is not interfered with and not to disconnect the software but check in the cockpit to see if the hi-jack button had been activated. That is most important. Only then should they disconnect the system from outside the fuselage to stop the engines and regain control of the aircraft".

"Great, simply great, we could not have publicised this incident anymore if we wanted to. The Press will love it, you can see the White House from the cockpit, and I'll bet the president was in residence."

He was right, the news channels worldwide made the most of it. The President promised a statement as soon as possible so Coltrane headed over to the White House and Stewart (Alistair) headed for his apartment.

Chapter Fifteen

Next morning Coltrane was in his office and received the news that the hijack button on the aircraft that had landed at Washington had been pressed. When interviewed the co-pilot admitted he had done that after being instructed to do so by a senior Boeing employee. He had been told it was a test drill not only of the software but the response and he was not to discuss it with anybody, not even his pilot in charge. He was adamant that the Boeing employee had shown him proof of his identity. He was given the exact time to press the hi-jack button which was located in the centre of the control panel and was equipped with a spring-loaded safety flap which he had to check went back in place after the button was pressed. He was told it was a full system check and he would be one of a few selected pilots who would then have a full working experience of the system. The co-pilot had not been told that this was all a set up and nothing to do with Boeing or any test. Coltrane understood immediately, very cleverly the hijackers had been able to stage a hijack without having to be on board the aircraft, but the result had been the same. An aircraft had been taken under their control and had landed remotely at a Washington airfield.

Coltrane began to find out if any of the engineers who had been working with Ray and Stewart had recently left the company and the list was short. Only one name, Ted McPherson had relocated from Seattle and not long after Ray and Stewart had moved Ted had been made redundant and had left the company. Coltrane had that gut feeling that almost certainly the Boeing employee who had approached the co-pilot Lew had been McPherson who probably still had his Boeing identity card or a very good copy. He had to update Allister (Stewart) so he rang Stewart's office number to be told that he had not arrived. Checking with the soldiers who were on duty at the apartment was worrying, his car was still parked in the garage but there was no sign of him. Normally they would have escorted him to his office for safety reasons. Coltrane did not wait, he drove over and found that the apartment was empty; the soldiers had checked the rear entrance to the apartment block which was supposed to remain locked and found it open. There was a trail of footprints across the grass and the security fence had been cut, Alistair had been kidnapped during the night. It looked as though it had been easy for them but for Coltrane it was a result, now he might find out with whom he was dealing when Alistair reported back. That was assuming he could get a message out somehow or escape.

He recalled his telephone conversation with Stewart the day before when Stewart had suggested that despite the demonstration whoever was responsible might still kidnap him because he was one of a few people with full knowledge of both systems. Alistair was in a dangerous position. If the people who had kidnapped him found out that they had the wrong brother, they might take drastic action. Back at his office there was a message for him that a police officer had brought in a man that he wanted to interview. The police officer was one of the pair who had come to their rescue when they had been attacked during the attempted kidnap two days previously. The man he had in custody was in his late twenties, tidily dress and confident, he was certain that no charges would be brought against him and repeatedly asked for his lawyer. Coltrane was having none of it.

"You were involved in the attempted kidnap of a CIA Agent who is involved in a serious terrorism case, that counts as treason and I don't need to give you access to a lawyer. If I don't get the answers, I need you will be detained indefinitely."

"You can't do that."

"Try me; I need to know who you were working for and the name and addresses of the others who were with you. You have five minutes to make a decision otherwise you are out of here and on the way to prison, a tough prison."

Coltrane walked out and left him, five minutes later he returned and got the information that he needed. One of the men had been contacted by email with instructions and full payment in cash promised beforehand; they had collected the money from a woman at a shop. They were local thugs looking for easy money, he arranged for the others to be brought in and charged with assault. It was not going well but he had options, so he returned to his office and made the decision to arrange for all the CIA software operators to have extra guards or be moved to a safer place. He realised that they were only trained to use the anti-hijack software, but he could not take any chances. Then there were the four operators that the military had hidden away that were fully trained on the latest software. If one of those four operators had been persuaded to carry out a remote-control takeover of the aircraft they would not have required any assistance from anyone on board, at least that is what he understood.

Finding the location of the operators who were able to deliberately take control of aircraft for safety reasons in the event of a hijack proved to be very difficult. He had to resort to calling Mercer and enlisting his help and even he was reluctant.

"Not sure if I can help, we have secure facilities that are used by all sorts of people and their location is not known to everybody. I will make a call and get somebody to call you back. Don't hold your breath."

Shortly afterwards Agent Bennett called him, and he explained what he needed.

"I hear you Agent Coltrane but am not able to help, we have two highly secure facilities one in the Rockies and the other in Hawaii. They are highly secure because they are complete communities, family homes, schools, and everything else. They are nice villages to live in, both with a population of around three hundred; I would like to live in one myself except you can't leave."

"Ever?"

"Only with a full security detail and you have to have a good reason. If you tried to add another layer of security, you would weaken the existing one."

"I just want to talk to the people that I have just described to you. All of them at both locations."

"Not possible but there is a way. Send me a written list of questions and I will send you their answers."

"Won't work, I need to interview them personally and try to get relevant answers."

"What you are saying is that you wish to interrogate them."

"Agent Bennett I am desperate for answers. Do you have a record of visitors to these four men?"

"Over how long?"

"Last three months." There was a long pause during which Coltrane could hear the sound of computer keys.

"No visitors, other than military or CIA."

Coltrane groaned that was an answer he had not considered.

"Do you have records of telephone calls, emails etc?"

"I do and I can help here, I can send you a list that covers the families of the four operators, it covers nine persons. We monitor all the ingoing and outgoing calls and emails."

"I look forward to receiving it."

"Later today."

Coltrane sank back in his chair; it was going to be a long slog. His intercom buzzed; it was his secretary.

"Washington Police Department, Chief Inspector Daniels on the line for you. Putting you through."

"Morning Chief Inspector, how can I help you?"

"Agent Coltrane we have recovered a body from a car park, it had a wallet in his pocket with an identity pass for Boeing. I called them and they said Stewart Phillips had relocated to your office building here in Washington. Do you know him?"

Coltrane went cold as he realised this was not Stewart, it was Alistair; He was carrying Stewarts identity cards.

"Yes, he works here. How did he die?"

"They dumped him on the top floor of a multi-story car park, legs and arms bound and a plastic bag over his head, it was taped in place. It was carried out by two men with covered faces, the car, a Honda, had its plates covered, we have a security camera recording but it does not help. There was an envelope fastened to his shirt front, we opened it and there was a brief message, it said 'DON'T TRY THIS AGAIN'. What does that mean?"

"No idea, I'll look into it."

Daniels sighed he knew the situation and that he would never get any answers, if the security services decided to keep it to themselves, he would be wasting his time trying to get answers.

"The body is in the city morgue; the coroner will deal with it. What address shall I put on the form?"

Coltrane gave him the apartment address and asked his secretary to fetch him a coffee. It had not taken them long to find out Alistair was the wrong brother. His main worry was where they going to teach them a lesson and take control of another aircraft. His second worry was that he had to tell Stewart. While he thought about that he called Mercer.

"It was a risk and Alistair knew it. I'll talk to the President while we brace ourselves against low flying aircraft." He rang off there was little else to say.

The list he had requested arrived from Bennett; it was formidable, so he put three agents on identifying the callers. It was going to take a long time.

Chapter sixteen.

A few days passed without any progress as Coltrane exhausted every lead without success. Stewart was shocked to learn that his brother had been murdered so soon after the kidnap. He regretted allowing Alistair to be involved as he had never thought that would help. It was only when Alistair had been so enthusiastic about being part of the deception that he began to realise his brother lead a life without excitement. Stewart returned home and moved back into the apartment, most of the time he worked from there but occasionally went into his office. Whether at the apartment, the office or driving he was heavily guarded, the CIA treated him as a precious asset. While away in hiding he had had been able to relax, now back at the apartment he was not sleeping, every little noise in the night woke him up. He would get up and without turning on any lights he would check the door and look out of the windows to see if the soldiers were still on guard. Often, he could not see anyone and began to panic until one walked out of the trees. Stewart knew that he had to train somebody to replace Ray; he did not for obvious reasons want to remain the only person with a total overview of the software.

He was in Coltrane's office where they were discussing how the hi-jackers had planned to take control of the aircraft and what were their objectives. Coltrane was repeating what he had said on many occasions.

"I think they just got lucky with that one hi-jack as the co-pilot was proud to be offered a chance to test a procedure that would save lives. The fact it is now some time since they landed that airliner at Ronald Regan and they haven't tried it again that points to luck."

Stewart was not sure and said so. Coltrane had received the report regarding the list that Bennet had supplied of all the contacts of the four operators and their families.

"Nothing obvious, there are a couple that we are still looking at, but I doubt if they will prove interesting."

Stewart had nothing to contribute.

"I have a team trying to get past the changed security on the software, we still do not know how they managed it but made changes to make it much harder for us to regain access."

"Will you be able to prevent them getting control again?"

"Definitely, I already have a security upgrade ready. When I get access, I will load it and they will not get in again. The upgrade will change the passwords and security procedure every day."

He had just finished speaking when Coltrane's secretary poked, her head through the door.

"Sir, turn your television on, quickly, any channel."

Stewart was nearest so he complied, the news announcer was repeating an earlier news cast.

"We have no further information on the breaking news story. Every nuclear armed country, there are nine of them, has received a message from a group calling themselves Global Action regarding the deployment of nuclear missiles. The White House has declined to comment at this stage."

Coltrane was dialling a number, even sitting on the other side of the desk Stewart heard the person who answered, it was Mercer. A brief conversation followed, and Coltrane was standing and throwing things into his briefcase, he pointed to the door as he switched off his phone.

"Get your things we are going to the White House." He called to his secretary.

"I need a car out front." They left with flashing lights and screaming sirens, it was only a short distance but there were traffic signals and plenty of traffic.

" Why the panic?"

"I only know the briefest details, let's wait until we get there but we are under threat."

When they arrived, they were shown to a briefing room where the President, the heads of NSA, the FBI and the CIA and representatives from the military were waiting.

The President waved them to chairs.

"Ah, we have the CIA agents who have been dealing with this situation, we will need their input. You will probably recognise agents Mercer, Steadman, and Coltrane; the fourth one I recognise is Stewart Phillips. He is seconded from Boeing."

Stewart found himself looking at the President again, it was daunting to be at that gathering.

The President coughed and while seated started to read from a sheaf of papers that he was holding.

"This morning, less than two hours ago, we received a communication from an organisation that is making demands on us, in particular on our nuclear capability. The document is headed Global Action, but that is not the name of the group. We do not know the name of the group, where they are based or the name of any individuals who are part of it. The same communication was sent to the governments of the other eight countries that have nuclear capability, it was also sent to the media in those countries. The media, as expected, reacted very quickly and it became a major news item around the world. We had barely had time to open the envelope before we were inundated with calls from the media, followed by the heads of state of the eight countries."

He paused and looked around the room before looking down at the papers that he was holding.

"The communication was not an agreement or a demand it was purely a statement that we have to comply with. It contains a threat that noncompliance will trigger a response that will result in the country concerned being targeted by multiple attacks by remotely controlled aircraft. The system to carry out those attacks is now under the total control of the authors of this document, there is no defence against such attacks. You will all know about the anti hi-jacking software that we developed, which became an offensive weapon. We did that because our dominance in nuclear technology had become eroded and we could see that a nuclear war was becoming a possibility. This new technology gave us the ability to take control of civilian airliners and use them as weapons, tens of thousands of weapons. Our opponents do not have any similar system which gives us the opportunity to control the military situation. Opposing countries have no defence and can be controlled by us having the opportunity to chastise them if they step out of line."

He stopped and looked around the room before continuing. "That opportunity came with a heavy responsibility; the safety of the world was in our hands. The situation changed dramatically when control of this software was taken from us by a group who has not identified themselves. It could be the government of one of the eight that I mentioned, or it could be another non-nuclear country, or it could be a terrorist group."

He waved the papers. "These do not help; we still do not know who we are dealing with."

One of the military men interrupted.

"What are they demanding?"

"That we decommission all our nuclear war heads."

The President had to raise his hand for silence as everybody tried to talk.

"We have five days to agree to this and fourteen days to start work."

"It's a joke."

"It is not a joke, last week an airliner landed at Ronald Reagan Airport a couple of miles from here and it was being flown by remote control, if it had overflown the airfield it would have landed where I am standing now. Similarly, the Pentagon, the Bank of America or the New York Stock Exchange could have been targeted, or one of our major car factories or power stations, nuclear or otherwise. Ten aircraft could bring this country to a standstill. We have no defence against this sort of attack, we can't use fighter jets or missiles, the only thing we can do is stop all flying and then they have no control over us but the economic consequences will be dramatic".

He paused for a drink of water.

"I think we have to agree to their demands. The Russian president was on the phone earlier enquiring whether the system for taking control of airliners was operational and that somebody other than us was in control of that system. Apparently, he was fully aware of the system and its potential. He indicated that they would agree to these demands provided we and China agree, if we do that the other six countries will have to agree."

Everyone around the table was thinking hard.

He held up copies of the Global Action communication.

"Please take a copy and read what they have to say. Let me know what you think. Of course, congress and the Senate will have their say but I feel that we must comply with the demands, we have little choice. I brought CIA agents Mercer, Steadman, Coltrane, and Phillips here so that you could question them. Please excuse me gentlemen."

He dropped his notes and the copies of the communication on the table and they all rose as he left the room.

The first question was from the head of the NSA.

"Realistically do we think you can take control back before the five days are up?"

"It's impossible, I think we have to do as the President suggests and agree to their demand."

The question was directed at the three of them, but Coltrane was answering for them all.

"Does Agent Phillips feel personally threatened, we understand that his brother was mistaken for him, taken hostage and murdered?"

"Agent Phillips is probably very safe; we are guarding him, also the group that we now regard as Global Action need him alive, so we are not expecting him to come to any harm in the near future despite what happened to his brother."

"Near future?"

"As this situation develops other parties may become aware of him and decide to kidnap him and take control of the software, that is the most serious threat to us and to him."

"As I understand it this software communicates with aircraft anywhere in the world. Does it use satellites to do that, in which case all we need to do is disable the satellites. I assume we are in control of them?"

"Yes, there are US military satellites, there are navigation satellites and destroying them will disable the navigation systems of aircraft and ships worldwide. There would be thousands of aircraft in trouble."

Stewart decided to intervene as the questions were not helping.

"Gentlemen, there isn't an easy solution, during the last few days we have considered every option and there are only a few possibilities, we are working on them and will keep you posted of any progress."

"Do you think we should know what those possibilities are?"

"No, I don't, if you will excuse us, we have a lot to do today."

He stood up and Coltrane, Mercer and Steadman followed him out of the room. Mercer was next to him and muttered.

"Well done, when they get started, they don't know when to stop."

When they exited the building, they were greeted by the sight of four Army trucks that were laden with soldiers. An Army officer advised Coltrane that there would be one truck in front and one truck behind each of their cars and that two other trucks had been despatched to the Phillip's apartment address to re-enforce the security already there. They were operating under orders from the President and it was a permanent situation.

Coltrane summed up the situation.

"No chance of meeting a lady for a quiet dinner date then."

Stewart was more concerned with what had been discussed at the meeting.

"I thought the President looked tired; this situation is putting a lot of stress on him."

"He's frightened."

"Do you see him often?"

"Every week, occasionally several times a week."

"Are you frightened?"

"I am bloody terrified, aren't you? This Global Action thing is deadly serious."

Stewart studied Coltrane and could see that he meant it.

"We'll beat them."

"I'm not sure, they have the upper hand and this demand will turn out to be the first of many. They will destabilise the world political and military situation. Of course, we would all like to see the end of war, but it cannot be done in a single stroke. The President feels the next demand could be for the removal of occupying forces from foreign lands. Just think how that will destabilise some volatile situations. The Middle East is only peaceful because of our presence in countries such as Iraq, Afghanistan, and Saudi Arabia, if we pull out of them all hell will break out. Similarly, we have a huge presence in Europe with our troops in England and Germany and many other countries. If we pulled out of there Russia would start flexing their muscles. Whoever these Global Action people are they are naive for thinking they can quickly change a situation that has taken a long time to evolve."

Chapter seventeen.

Back at the CIA building Stewart found that his office had moved, it had gone up two floors and he was now across the corridor from Coltrane. They sat down in Coltrane's office.

"I take it that you do have lines of inquiry that you are pursuing. Do you need help; you can have anything that you need?"

"I would prefer to be left alone at present but that doesn't mean that other CIA agents should not be trying to find out who Global Action is. I just don't want them under my feet."

"Understood."

Stewart went across the corridor to his own office and carefully closed the door. His mind was in turmoil, he had several ideas, but he needed to think. On his desk was a copy of the list that had been provided by Bennett, it was covered in pencil notes. It was almost complete, they had checked every call and message and there were none that were suspicious, but he had not expected it to be that easy. He immediately noticed some calls that were circled and noted as no longer in use, they had not been able to check those, they were all to a Sergeant Fisher. What had attracted his attention was that they were from Alan Chapman and Ted McPherson, Angel's husband was Alan Chapman and McPherson was an employee of Boeing in Seattle when he was there. Stewart remembered that he and Ray had voiced a few concerns about him and a short time later he had left. He called Boeing and spoke to his old boss who remembered McPherson.

"He moved to Washington left about the time you moved there."

"Do you know where he went?"

"No, why are you interested in him."

"Not sure but I'm enquiring into some unusual activity regarding the software that I am working on."

"We fired him; it was reported to me that he was looking into projects that he was not authorised to have access to."

"Would that include the software that Ray and I had developed?"

"Could be, I am not certain."

Stewart thanked him and crossed the corridor to Coltrane's office; he was on the phone but cut the call as soon as he saw Stewarts face.

"Something interesting just come up, that list of contacts that Bennett gave us has two contacts that are now unavailable. One is Alan Chapman who you may remember was married to Angel Krasinski."

"I remember her, have you had your way with her yet? No wait a moment her former husband died."

"Five years ago."

"Calls from him now doesn't mean he is alive. Somebody may have his phone."

"Or did have it, it's no longer in use. We must talk to Angel. There is a second man with a dead phone." He explained about McPherson.

"Could he have read your notes?" Stewart had to think.

"I locked my notes away every night, but they would be on my desk in the day but I'm thinking that he may have tapped into my computer terminal. Ray and I never quite understood what his role was and we both found him to be a little bit odd. I discussed this with Ray and shortly afterwards MacPherson was dismissed."

"Right we must find him, and we need further research into those two phones. The phone companies will help. "

"Shall we send somebody over to the FAA to pick Angel up, we can't really go ourselves. If we do, we will have two Army trucks and forty soldiers with us."

"Not necessarily, I have a pool car in the rear car park; will take another agent with me and go out of a different exit as I am not sure if the army are following me. The Army depend on us to tell them when we are going somewhere."

The FAA offices were on the other side of the city. Coltrane was concerned with protocol.

"We can't just walk in and speak to her we must speak to her supervisor first."

The supervisor was a strict looking woman who met them in the entrance hall.

"Mrs Chapman doesn't work here anymore."

"You know her as Chapman?"

"She was Miss Krasinski when she joined us but changed it to Chapman. Her employment record says Krasinski but everything else is in the name of Chapman."

"When did she leave?"

"We don't know, she missed work and we thought she might be ill and would let us know when she was ready. She was not taking any calls so after a week I sent somebody to her home to see if she was alright, she lived in Falls Church. There was nobody there, it was empty, and neighbours she had moved out. We could find her if we wanted to but we have an outstanding salary payment so we figured she would get in touch."

Coltrane was a bit puzzled as Angel was on a watch list and here movements should have been monitored.

Back in the office Coltrane told Stewart what had happened and asked the question that was troubling him.

"What do you make of that?"

"There are too many loose ends and I get the feeling that they will all join up one day."

Coltrane's phone rang it was Mercer.

"Where are you?"

"At the office."

"We are needed at the White House as soon as possible."

"I'll be there".

"Bring Stewart with you."

Stewart heard the conversation, and together they went down to the front entrance and were walking towards Coltrane's car when an Army officer confronted them.

"Sir, if you are going out you should advise us first."

"Sorry, we are going to the White House."

"You will have to park in the main car park; the visitor parking is too small for our trucks."

"We'll park in the visitor's park and you can decide where you will park."

The meeting was in the same room as the last one and the same people were present. The President arrived through another door as they entered the room. He looked a little drawn. Everybody sat down but he remained standing.

"Gentlemen, its three days since we were here last, and we have to comply with the requirements of the communication from Global Action. We have decided to agree, it has been discussed by all those that have a legal right to share their opinion. There are those, me included, that believe we should agree and there are a few other that do not. They have a genuine fear that it might be the wrong decision. Despite that we have a unanimous agreement that we send a message of compliance. We have been in contact with the leadership of Russia, China, Pakistan, Israel, India, France and the United Kingdom and they will be doing the same. We have been unable to speak to the leadership of North Korea; they do not answer our messages and they appear to be ignoring Global Actions request. As far as we know they have about ten nuclear warheads out of a world total of sixteen thousand, so we might find out what will happen to North Korea if they dissent."

The President paused,

"Global Action, we are using that name in the absence of any other, hasn't provided us with an address so the only way to advise them that we agree is to use the press. We will issue a release to the media associations tomorrow; therefore, we will be within their five days' notice period. The other countries that I mentioned are doing the same. That is except for North Korea, we are not sure what they are doing. Do you have any questions?" There were none.

Chapter eighteen.

The next day the press went crazy with television news taking control. There were special programmes with a line-up of experts commenting for or against the decision. They covered the decision of each country and in the beginning did not appear to notice that North Korea had not said yes or no. It was only when the five-day deadline expired that they concentrated on that country. As the television services of most countries did not have a correspondent in North Korea they had to rely on 'expert' opinion. These discussions were interrupted by a news flash.

"We are receiving news of an aircraft incident at Pyongyang, the capital of North Korea. A Tupolev TU 204 of state airline Air Koryo failed to take-off from Sunan International Airport. There are no reports regarding casualties."

Stewart's phone rang it was Coltrane.

"Have you seen the news? There has been an airliner crash in North Korea."

"That's interesting, but it did not actually crash it just failed to take off"

"Could be a normal flying accident."

"It could but you and I don't think so, do we?"

Stewart went across to Coltrane's office which had a television; there were two other people there. They were all talking and offering some opinions.

The programme was interrupted by a second news flash.

"We are receiving news of a second aircraft incident in North Korea. An airliner belonging to national carrier Air Koryo has failed to take off at Orang Airport in the north of the country close to the Sea of Japan. There are no reports regarding casualties."

Coltrane was the first to speak.

"Two incidents, one after another, they are not a co-incidence."

As he finished speaking his phone was ringing, he pointed at it before picking it up.

"That will be the White House." He was right.

They were there within fifteen minutes, same room but some extra people. This time they had to wait for the President. He was talking as he entered the room.

"Gentlemen, it looks like we made the right decision. The North Koreans initially denied there was a problem but with two runways blocked by stationary aircraft, one at the capital and the other in the north they will have to rethink their decision."

"Mr President why are stationary aircraft important?"

"The North Koreans did not put them there, they were remotely controlled and while they are there, they cannot use the runways, the airports are closed."

"Surely they can tow them out of the way?"

"Those two aircraft have their brakes on, and their engines are still running, the ground crew won't attach a towing vehicle to them until the engines are shutdown. The risk is that whoever put them there could apply full throttle and push the towing vehicle down the runway, I don't need to remind you that there are probably several hundred passengers on those two aircraft."

"Have we any idea how long they will stay there?"

Stewart answered that one.

"Could be until the fuel runs out. They were departing so there will be plenty in the tanks, could be five or six hours, it depends on where they were going."

Coltrane spoke quietly.

"It was a lesson; nobody was hurt but North Korea now understands the situation."

There was obviously going to be some lengthy discussion which Stewart and himself could not contribute to so Coltrane requested that they be excused.

The President had one question for them.

"Do you in your opinion and for the record consider this is the work of those people that we refer to as Global Action?"

"Definitely and it emphasises how careful we have to be when we deal with them."

When they arrived back at Coltrane's office, they were met by his secretary who had a note for him he read it and passed it to Stewart. It was a copy of a message from the United Nations to the President advising him that North Korea was blaming the United States for the hi-jackings that had occurred in North Korea. No further details were given.

"They were quick."

"Predictable."

"Will we be involved in this?"

"Definitely not, we stay out of it. I will make that clear to Mercer. What, specifically are you working on?"

"I am trying to find Ted McPherson."

"The guy who worked at Boeing?"

"He was working at Boeing when I joined, never had much to do with him but he was always about in the office. He was a software programmer and worked on software for improving flight efficiency."

"Why are you interested in him?"

"I inquired to my old boss at Renton as to why he left."

"He said he was dismissed for breaching his terms of employment, and they don't know who he went to work for. Which seems a little curious and when I think back, he was always a little curious about my work."

"Could he have learned anything about it?"

"To be truthful, in that office we were always a bit easy going when we should not have been."

"Could he have found out some detail?"

"Every desk had a small safe for storing documents overnight. But now, when I think back there were times during the day when he was in the office on his own. It is probably nothing but I just have a feeling that I should check him out. Also he might have compromised my computer terminal, and I think we should find Angel."

"I'll do that when I get back. I'm meeting some guys from the National Security Agency (NSA)."

"You're going to Baltimore."

"Hell no, they are coming here."

"You're honoured."

With a coffee from the machine at the end of the corridor Stewart settled down for some quiet thinking. But he did not make any progress, there were too many unanswered questions, how had they taken control of the two aircraft over North Korea if the hi-jack button on board had not been pressed? Surely all pilots would have been informed that any suggestions of testing should be ignored. Money and threats must have been used and he was no further forward when Coltrane returned.

"How did that go?"

"They can tell you themselves, they will be here shortly they want to see what our security arrangements are like."

"We are in a CIA office for goodness sake, we should be secure."

They arrived a few minutes later both were smartly dressed and introduced themselves as Nick Powell and Alex Pendry and did not waste any time. After the usual pleasantries Agent Pendry made it clear they were not happy with the reliance being placed on the guards at the reception desk.

"We are solely responsible for the safety of Stewart Phillips and feel that the present arrangements are inadequate. If somebody got into this building the security guards would not be able to protect him."

Coltrane was quick to speak.

"They would not be coming here to harm him; they would be here to abduct him. Getting in might be possible but getting him out would be a difficult matter."

"I am fully briefed on this matter and as I understand it, if they already had a replacement for Agent Phillips, they could decide to eliminate him. That way they would have everything they needed, and we would have no access to the software."

Stewart felt he had to intervene.

"In a situation such as that they could simply kill me anywhere, shoot me as I get out of the car. No need for them to get into this office block."

"Whatever, we have decided that personal protection is the answer so we are allocating three specialists, two of them, will be with you at all times. We have inspected your apartment and the situation is the same, wire fencing is not good protection. They have already cut that and timed patrols around the estate are futile. You have spare bedrooms at your apartment so the security specialists will move in with you; the army unit will stand down. When you go out, either from here or the apartment one of the three will go first and check outside and the car. You will have three cars at your disposal, and you will use them on different occasions. When you leave the apartment one of the specialists will remain behind to watch over it. When you leave this office the security guards here will position one guard outside your office for the duration while you are away."

Coltrane and Stewart were astounded.

"You're kidding us."

"We are not, we considered putting you in a safe house where you could work and sleep but you are required at other places, including the White House from time to time so that was unworkable."

Stewart knew he should be grateful for the effort to keep him safe.

"What will these specialists do during the time I am working here at my office?"

"You have large office so your secretary can move in with you; all she will need is a desk and chair."

"I don't have a secretary."

"You do now."

"What will she do all day?"

"I don't know, read a book or solve a crossword. It does not matter so long as she keeps an eye on you. The second specialist that will travel with you each day will keep an eye on your car while it is parked here."

Both Coltrane and Stewart realised that nothing was open for discussion and Pendry knew that.

"Is everything clear and understood? The three agents will move into your apartment when you get back there."

Agents Powell and Pendry left and they moved over to Stewarts office, as they did so two men appeared with a desk, a table and two chairs. They moved Stewarts desk and placed the second desk with its chair in a position directly facing the door. The table and second chair were placed in the corridor for the guard.

"I don't believe this, but we won't complain." Coltrane shook his head in disbelief.

Coltrane received a steady stream of messages.

"We've located Angel, she's at her parents' house in Baltimore, says she had had enough of the FAA and decided to quit and move out of Washington."

"There's more to it than that."

"She had kept Chapman's phone; no idea why and even paid the bills."

"For five years?"

Coltrane shrugged.

"Woman thing."

Stewart was curious.

"Who questioned her?"

"Local agent, we sent the questions."

"Did he ask her if she knew Ted McPherson?"

"Said she had never heard of him."

"What about Fisher, the operator that we can't meet?"

"Never heard of him."

"Her phone number was on the list that Bennett supplied."

"She's lying."

Coltrane was deep in thought. "We will have to go to Baltimore and talk to her ourselves but first we want to talk to Fisher."

"Bennett insists that it isn't possible."

"We have to make it possible, either they take us to him, or they bring him to a neutral meeting point, their choice. I'll speak to Mercer and he can sort it out, we have access as far up as the President so it should be possible."

Coltrane's secretary brought him head shots of Alan Chapman and Ted McPherson.

Coltrane explained, "I ordered these earlier, I felt these two were interesting, but we did not know what they looked like."

Stewart glanced at the photos. "Which is which, hang on these are the same person but taken in different places." Coltrane took the photographs from him.

"Are you sure."

He studied the images again. "You're right it is the same person."

"I'll tell you something else. That isn't McPherson or at least it's not the man who was at Boeing who called himself McPherson when I was there."

Chapter nineteen.

Coltrane was on the phone to Mercer when he left; he waved from the door and headed for the front entrance. He was supposed to advise security in advance that he was leaving but was interested in finding out how the new arrangements would work. The entrance was busy, so he was surprised as he exited the elevator when he was approached and identified as Stewart Phillips. He was immediately cautious, but the man had an identity tag around his neck, the tag identified him as CIA and a visitor. He was very polite.

"Good afternoon Mr Phillips, I'm part of your new security arrangements, there are three of us who are tasked with your personal safety. I am Darren Askin and my colleague Aaron Lewis is outside keeping a watch on the car park. The third member of the team is Rosie Cooke; she is already at your apartment overseeing the handover from the army security. Where are you heading now?"

"My apartment, I have a car here."

"We realise that, if you let me have the keys, I will arrange for it to be collected. May I ask if you carry a weapon?"

"I have a revolver but not with me."

"Please do not carry it." Stewart was relieved to hear him say that as Ray had been killed by his own gun, he acknowledged that weapons were not one of his skills.

Darron used a portable radio to contact his colleague in the car park to advise him they were leaving. They got into the car and Darren introduced him to Aaron.

"What do we call you Sir?"

"Well I'm Agent Phillips of course but everybody knows me as Stewart."

"Stewart, you will always travel in the back and there will always be two of us with you. The third member of our team will remain at your apartment while we are away. We have several cars and they are fully equipped for our task; their movement can be monitored, and we carry a variety of weapons for defensive purposes. We change roles from time to time so you will not always travel with the same operatives. If we encounter any trouble, we expect you to obey any orders that we give, without delay."

"I'm impressed." He was also curious about Aaron's role.

"Have you been sitting in the car all the time that I have been here?"

Aaron laughed and explained that the car had been under surveillance by a camera which he had watched in the security guard's office.

"I walk out and physically check it every thirty minutes."

Stewart was surprised at the thoroughness of the security.

"Why do you pay so much attention to the car?"

"We were told that you were just as likely to be abducted as actually attacked. The best way to abduct somebody is to be sitting in their car and waiting for them."

They pulled out of the car park and it was a pleasant drive to the apartment.

"So, you don't resort to flashing lights and sirens?"

"We have those, but they are out of sight and we would only use them in an emergency. The local police are aware of us and can find us quickly by using our tracking devices. If we need assistance they will be here quickly."

Stewart settled down and decided that this was the best way to get around in Washington. The ride gave him the opportunity to study the two agents in the front seats. They were dressed in casual clothes that were not new and would not attract attention. He quickly noticed that they did not talk a lot, they concentrated on their job, and it was comforting. While he had never had cause to feel unsafe when Coltrane was driving, he definitely felt safer with these two. His thoughts highlighted to him the precarious situation that he found himself in. They turned into the entrance of the gated community and the barrier was raised without them having to identify themselves, the guards there had obviously been briefed. The army trucks had gone, and a gardener was trying to rectify the damage to the lawn that had been caused by the soldiers. Aaron radioed up to the agent in the apartment who confirmed that everything was as it should be, and they used the elevator to reach the apartment. The door was opened by a slender woman who was about the same age and build as Darren and Aaron, he decided he would not take her on in a fight. She was introduced as Rosie. Considering everything he realised he was stuck with the three of them for some time, but it could have been worse. Rosie seemed to take charge.

"Sir, we will obviously establish a routine but for now I have made some arrangements."

"Please call me Stewart."

"Stewart, I have done some shopping for breakfast things, I checked what you had in the kitchen, so I bought more of the same. We will have breakfast here and when you leave one of us will stay here. I assume you will have lunch at your office and after you return one of us will go for a takeaway. That is unless there is something you prefer in which case; we will do some shopping. I have arranged for a cleaning company to come here twice a week to tidy up and do the washing. Their cleaners are security checked and carry out the same services for all the CIA offices and buildings in the Washington area."

Stewart was beginning to feel trapped but knew he was secure.

"Any questions?"

"Do we have anybody outside?"

"We have three agents in one of the apartments below us; it was not in use, so we took control of it. They will be here around the clock watching the outside of the building and the parking area."

They all agreed on a fish supper and Aaron arranged to collect it at seven o'clock.

As they were finishing their meal, they received a message that a car with a single occupant had entered the parking area and a man was approaching their building. With a minute the man was identified as Agent Coltrane and a couple of minutes after that he was admitted to the apartment.

"Sorry about disturbing you but I have received a message from Agent Bennett."

Everybody was looking around for answers, but Stewart knew exactly who it was and it was either good news or bad news.

"He has arranged for us to meet Fisher tomorrow. He will be on a Gulfstream jet that will land at Dulles Airforce base at approximately three in the afternoon. We can talk to him for an hour and he will bring proof of his identity with him. I asked for that in case somebody tried to deceive us."

"We don't need that; I can tell in a few minutes if he knows what he is talking about."

Coltrane was smiling.

"They've been clever, we still won't know where he is based. Also, I have arranged for Angel to be picked up for questioning, we can talk to her at Baltimore. I was tempted to have her brought here but we can have a look at her parents place while we are there."

"Or anything else that comes out of talking to her."

Stewart was certain something would.

"Can you ask the local office to see if Alan Chapman or Ted McPherson live in the Baltimore area?"

"Will do, see you in the morning."

Chapter twenty.

Next day Stewart was escorted to his car and driven over to collect Coltrane when they arrived at Dulles Airport the Gulfstream carrying Fisher had already arrived and was parked away from the airport buildings. Arron escorted them to the airport security office and they were taken out to the aircraft. As they approached, they could see two airport vehicles parked near it and several suited men walking around it. Coltrane commented.

"Typical overkill."

As they approached the aircraft two men intercepted them, they were CIA agents and they inspected their identity cards before allowing them access to the steps up to the aircraft. Stewart had never been inside a corporate jet aircraft before and was immediately impressed by how luxurious it was. The cabin was fitted with luxurious seats and small tables for eight passengers, there were two men on board. A quick glance forward towards the cockpit showed it to be empty.

The two occupants in the cabin were dressed in casual suits and were smiling, neither stood up to greet them but one introduced himself.

"Afternoon, I take it you are Coltrane and Phillips, I am Agent Bennett, and this is Agent Fisher."

Neither Stewart nor Coltrane had been expecting Bennett to be there himself but they understood he was based in Washington and assumed he was there to find out what was going on. They sat across the table from the other two and Stewart opened the conversation, before any general discussion he wanted to verify that Fisher was one of the operators.

"How long have you been on this duty?"

"Five years."

"A comfortable life from what I hear, choice of Hawaii or Las Vegas."

"Comfortable yes but don't know about Hawaii or Las Vegas."

He was not giving anything away about his base except for a small smile.

"Where you fully training including how to taxi aircraft?"

"I was trained to taxi but have never done so, it is risky as we do not have any forward vision unlike drone remote control pilots who have a camera looking forwards. Airliners do not have this facility and to taxi using charts runs the risk of putting a wheel on the grass. A two hundred ton or more aircraft would sink very quickly. We take control of an aircraft when it has left the ground usually fifty feet or more but personally, I think that is risky. When landing an aircraft, we stop on the runway and leave it there for ground crew to tow it to a parking place."

He was giving the correct answers, Stewart had expected that.

"Did you ever have any problems with the software?"

"Not really, in the beginning we had some learning issues and a quick call to Boeing resolved them. I would talk to Ray Wheeler, he was most helpful, how is he by the way?"

"Dead, he was shot."

That shook him.

"What happened?"

Stewart chose to ignore the question and moved on.

"How many airliners have you remotely hi-jacked?"

Bennett coughed as though to say that was a question that Fisher could not answer. Fisher accepted the warning and commented.

"Ray was a great guy, technically and good company."

"You met him?"

"Yes, I was over at Renton, you were there."

Stewart did not remember him, but it was an opportunity to identify Fisher with certainty.

"Was that when the software developers were in the production building?"

"Were they ever in that building? I would have liked to see the planes being screwed together but only got as far as that other building where the software guys lived?"

He had been there, Stewart decided he was genuine, and Coltrane shared that view judging from the arched eyebrows.

"What exactly did you want to ask me, why am I here?"

"We want to ask you about phone calls that you received from callers who we would prefer you not talk to."

Fisher sighed. "I expect you mean that bloody woman. She called me late one night and we had a short conversation."

"Who was she?" Stewart suspected he already knew the answer.

"Don't know, she did not say and when I asked, she ignored the question."

"What did she want?"

"She asked if I would do something for her. It paid two million dollars and would take a few hours."

"My first reaction was that she was some sort of idiot."

"Where were you when she called?"

"At home. She told me to think about it and she would call me at the same time the next day, which she did. She said she had a bank draft in my name for two million dollars which I could pay into any bank. She said it was like cash, if I wanted to keep it quiet, I could open an account at a foreign bank."

"Were you interested?"

"That is what she asked, and I said yes, who would not, I was curious. She said somebody else would call me the next day and explain. Before she hung up, I asked her again who she was, and she did not answer. Afterwards I rang the number from the list of incoming calls on my phone and it was not answered. The next day a man rang and explained that he wanted me to remotely hi-jack an airliner and that no one on board would be in danger. I pretended that I did not know what he was talking about, but he knew differently he understood how the inti hi-jacking system and the military version both worked and who I was and that two million dollars would be a nice earner. I told him he was mistaken, and I was not interested to which he replied that I should think about it and he would call next day."

The expression on Bennetts face showed that he did not know anything about these calls.

"You should have reported these calls."

"I know that, but I did not."

"Did he call the next day?"

"Yes, he explained that he wanted an airliner to be taken over, a specific airliner at an exact time when the hi-jack button on board would be operated and it was to be flown to Washington Ronald Regan Airport. I was to land it there and nobody would be hurt. I asked him some questions, but he did not answer any of them. I told him I was not interested, and he was very calm as he explained that I had a lovely family, a wife and two daughters and four grandparents."

"Implying some serious actions."

"You better believe it."

"So, what happened?"

"Nothing I had no further contact with him or the woman."

"You did not take control of an airliner for him?"

"I've just said I did not."

"Well somebody did, it took off from Las Vegas destined for Chicago, left its intended route and went to Ronald Regan, made a perfect landing and turned onto a taxiway and stopped."

Stewart was watching him carefully; his head came up quickly and he spoke without thinking.

"It stayed on the runway."

He knew he had made a mistake and attempted to explain.

"I saw it on the TV news, and it was on the runway."

Stewart continued to stare at him as he dropped his gaze to the floor.

"We all know that you were in control of that aircraft."

There was a pause and he nodded his head.

"I was a fool; the money was tempting but the decider was when he threatened my family."

"Did you hear from him again?"

"Oh yes, he wanted two more aircraft to be controlled in North Korea."

"We know about these."

"I said I was definitely not interested. His reply was that I could not back out or I was finished. He offered me a deal. Carry out the North Korea plan and teach him the protocols for using the system. If I did that, I would get the two million dollars, and nothing would be said about my involvement. I accepted."

The three of them, Coltrane, Bennett, and Stewart were aghast.

"Please tell us that you did not disclose the protocols to him."

"It doesn't matter, the security codes can be changed to keep him out."

"The security codes have been changed, the other controllers, and me can't access the software. He is now the only person who can do that, he is completely in control."

Stewart was furious and Fisher went very pale as he realised the situation. Bennett was beside himself.

"You fool do you know what you have done.?"

Coltrane opened his brief case and produced the photographs of Alan Chapman and Ted McPherson.

"Despite saying you never met him you obviously did. Which one of these men did you meet?"

Fisher studied the photographs for a moment before saying.

"Could be either of them, it's difficult to be certain because he had a beard."

"Colour, close cropped or bushy?"

"It was black like his hair and bushy."

Coltrane looked at Bennett. "We'll leave him to you."

"It will be a pleasure; he will be well looked after. Please ask the agents outside to come aboard."

With that Stewart and Coltrane left the aircraft and walked back to their car. Coltrane dialled a number and Stewart recognised the name of the person that he asked for, he was Agent in Charge at Baltimore CIA office.

"Chris, you still have Angelica Krasinski in custody, good, will you bring her parents in for questioning and will you secure their house and property, excellent, twenty-four hour guard, nobody goes in and the Krasinski's mustn't take anything with them. Just the clothes they are wearing. We will be with you in Baltimore tomorrow morning"

Stewart was not sure what Coltrane was up to. "Do you think her parents are involved?"

"No, but a little pressure helps. That woman is involved and can tell us a lot. We now know more than we did but cannot use it yet. If we put a big effort into finding who is behind this, he will find out and retaliate, more aircraft will be making unscheduled landings."

Chapter twenty-one.

After an early start Stewart and Coltrane made it to Baltimore by nine o'clock despite the early morning commuter traffic. Coltrane had been to the CIA offices before and was able to direct the driver straight to a parking spot. They had discussed the way that they would approach Angel and had decided that they would look fresh and relaxed; she on the other hand would have had a couple of nights in a cell. They decided to interview her for an hour and then without telling her they would look at her parents' house. That way if there was anything that she told them that was at her parents' house they could pick it up before they continued their interview. The guard looked through the spy hole and unlocked the door; Stewart pushed it open with his toe. She was standing there in yellow prison overalls which were many sizes too big for her. It was not necessary for her to be in prison garb, but it would help with their interview strategy. Her hair was a complete mess and it was obvious that she had not slept well. Stewart advanced into the cell with Coltrane behind him, both had coffee cups in their hand; they had not brought one for Angel. The cell was a square concrete box with a single window which was barred on the outside. On the left was a single bunk which was fixed to the wall and on the right was a toilet and washbasin. There was a screen that provided some privacy for the toilet; it just hid it from the view from the spy hole when the occupant was seated.

"Hi Angel, how are you?"

She could barely answer because she had filled up with emotion and she spoke quietly.

"Not very good, why are you keeping me here in this horrible place?"

Stewart looked around.

"This isn't bad compared with where you are going if you don't tell us what we need to know."

"You're going to keep me locked up?

While they were talking Coltrane had moved behind Stewart and crossed to the toilet. He cautiously raised the seat with his toe and peered inside. He let it fall back and when he turned, he had a disgusted expression on his face, and he looked down at Angel's lower half. It was an old ploy that unsettled female prisoners. Apparently if female guards did it to male prisoners it did not have any effect. It worked in Angel's case from the expression on her face he could see that she felt violated. He took a long drink from his coffee and suggested that the interview room would be a more comfortable place to talk. Two guards escorted them to a bare windowless room with just a table and four chairs.

She sat down and he suspected she was willing to do anything to avoid going back to the cell. Coltrane asked the guard to bring another coffee.

"What do you want to know?"

"Everything. Tell us how you became involved with Global Action?"

"Global Action, I don't know what that is?"

"Sorry my mistake, we received a demand from an organisation that was headed with those words, but they did not identify themselves, so we call them Global Action."

"I see what you mean, they did not identify themselves because they are not an entity and they are not an organisation. We are individuals with a common cause."

"Why do you do that?"

"You have no organisation to strike back at and we have the best opportunity to achieve our aims."

"Which are?"

"To bring about global disarmament, we are sliding towards a major war."

"Another 'save the world' group."

"Don't sneer, the world is a very dangerous place at the moment."

"Let's start by telling me about Alan Chapman."

"Allan was nothing to do with this he was just my husband. We had been married a couple of years when we decided on a walking holiday in Mexico where we met up with other walkers. One was Ted McPherson who it turned out had similar views to myself about nuclear weapons, views that I had formed at university. For three weeks we went everywhere together until one day we were at the coast climbing down some rocky cliffs and Alan slipped and fell. Ted managed to get down to him, but he was unable to get him out of the water, and I could not get a cell phone signal to ask for help. The tide was going out, so we had to do something. Our car was parked a couple of miles along the cliff, so I went for help. When I got back Alan's body had been taken out to sea and Ted had not been able to prevent it. We stayed for a long time, but his body was never found, sometimes I thought that the authorities did not believe me, and they thought that Ted was my husband. Anyway, we came back, I lived in Washington and Ted lived in Seattle and worked at Boeing, but we kept in touch. Ted was moved to Washington and on one occasion one of my neighbours said she was pleased that my husband had returned. They were very alike, same height and hair colour, same build. One day Ted asked if he could become my husband as he had some issues that he needed to walk away from."

"What were they?"

"He never said."

"So, he became Alan Chapman, your husband."

"Yes, he had plenty of money and I did not, so it was a good solution."

"Which was why we could not find him when he left, he had disappeared."

Coltrane produced the two photographs and showed them to her. She identified the Alan Chapman image but struggled with the second one.

"That could be either of them but Ted has a beard now."

"Do you have any photographs of him with the beard?"

"Somewhere, I would have to search."

"Carry on, what happened next?"

"Everything was normal, married life I mean. Occasionally we would talk about nuclear weapons it was a common interest. At that time North Korea, you know Kim, was creeping into the news and it was obvious that he was going to be trouble. Suddenly Alan, I mean Ted had a plan to sort it all out. It involved a programmer who was moving from Boeing Renton Plant to Washington and he told me to get to know him. "She looked directly at Stewart. "That was you of course."

Stewart began to understand why he had always felt uncomfortable with McPherson, the man had a dual identity, by day he was Ted and at home he was Alan

"Then you changed your mind, you left your job at the FAA and sold your house in Washington, what happened?"

"It was no one thing but a lot of small things. I think I probably knew them from the start but ignored them."

Tears were streaming down her face.

"I began to think that Alan did not fall on that cliff face in Mexico."

She paused and they had to wait for her to continue.

"I think Ted pushed him and when he climbed down to him Alan was still alive and when I went for help, he went down again and finished him off and pushed him into the sea."

She struggled with the last sentence and Stewart felt sorry for her.

"Do you think Ted had planned this from the beginning?"

They had to wait for her reply. "Yes."

"You said you might have a photograph of Ted McPherson; will that be at your parents' house?"

"All my stuff is there."

"I think you have told us a lot but not everything, we are on our way there to take a look."

"Please don't go there my mother isn't very strong."

"Both your mother and father are here we were planning to interview them when we got back from their house."

She completely broke down.

"When we get back, we will talk to you first before interviewing them, give us the right answers and we won't bother with them."

"You're all bastards, you two and McPherson."

Her parents' house was only a couple of miles away; it was a caravan trailer on a trailer park. Some trailer parks were reasonable this one was not, there was rubbish, car tyres and wrecked cars everywhere.

Coltrane was the first to comment. "She must have been really upset to leave Falls Church for this."

They found the correct trailer easily as there was a police car and saloon parked outside; each of them had two occupants. The two police officers approached them first and were joined by the CIA agents from the saloon. They identified themselves and the police officers left, the CIA men had the keys to the trailer. The trailer was in good condition, everything was freshly painted including the gate posts. Looking around Stewart decided it was the best one he could on the park. There was a Ford pick-up on the pathway and that seemed to be in good order, obviously Angel's father took good care of everything. The inside was the same; Coltrane looked around and sniffed the air.

"I've been in a lot of these things and they usually smell pretty bad; this is a good one."

They searched everywhere including under the trailer itself and found nothing that was interesting. In a kitchen cupboard the found some cardboard folders with personal papers in them relating to the old couple.

"We'll take them with us, we can check out the bank accounts."

Surprisingly, there was no computer equipment, they could understand that the old couple might not be into technology but expected Angel herself to have at least basic stuff. Coltrane was studying the electrical wall sockets.

"They are all in use except the two over by the window; whatever was in there was removed."

"Possibly a laptop and a printer?"

They went outside and looked around; there was a small lock up garage on the other side of the street. It was in good repair and the woodwork was the same colour as some of the fittings on the trailer. When they tried to open the garage door, they found it was locked solid from the inside. There was a smaller door on the side, and this had three locks. Coltrane was already walking back to the trailer. "They've got something in there that they don't want to lose."

They searched everywhere without success and concluded that the keys must be hidden outside.

Coltrane was putting some glass jars back in a cupboard when there was a jingling sound. The jar held rice and when they tipped it out, they found a set of keys. The side door to the garage opened easily and revealed a well laid out office, two desks and a filing cabinet and a modern computer set up.

Stewart sat at one desk and asked the question, "Why are there two desks?"

"McPherson must have spent time here."

Stewart was searching the draws and found some letters one was signed Abe Krasinski and it was addressed to a woman in Los Angeles and they were discussing nuclear disarmament.

"Her parents are involved."

In a drawer in the other desk they found a diary and an address book, they belonged to Angel. Every drawer on the filing cabinet was full of files relating to government military activity.

One file dealt with emails to several contacts in Iran.

"This is too much for us; we need a team up here to go through it."

"She might have appeared to be just a long-legged blond but it's obvious that she was more than that."

Coltrane found an empty cardboard box and threw some things into it including the diary and address book and some letters from each desk and the filing cabinet.

"These will do for now, let's see what she says about them."

They went outside and waved the two agents over; they were sitting in their car.

"Don't worry about the trailer you are to guard this garage, it's locked, and nobody is to go near it. We'll send a team up here shortly to search it."

He pocketed the keys and they drove away.

Chapter twenty-two.

They decided that they would not mention the garage to Angel at first and only bring it into the discussion if they did not get the answers that they needed from her.

"Stewart can you take the lead in the interview, you seem to have a talent for it?"

This was a complete surprise to Stewart as he had never been trained in interviewing. After a few minutes thought he realised that Coltrane wanted to remain in the background and intervene at the end. He was confrontational sometimes and it produced results.

Angel was pleased to see them.

"Anything you want me to explain?"

"We don't think so, we did not find anything in the trailer." He held up the folder that they had found in a kitchen cupboard. There has not been time for us to look at the bank statements in here. Your mother and father weren't money laundering or anything like that."

"If we were into that do you think we would be living in a trailer on that crummy trailer park?"

It occurred to Stewart that if they had not noticed the garage, they would have believed her and perhaps been sympathetic.

"Tell us about your husband?"

"Which one?"

"The current one."

"I've told you all that I know about him, we met him on holiday in Mexico."

"Where did he live when you met him?"

"Near Seattle when he was working at Boeing."

"Do you have an address?" She thought for a while before saying she could not remember it.

"As you haven't found anything are you releasing my mother and father?"

"We might do if you start telling us about McPherson." She sighed indicating that she regarded them as a nuisance.

"I genuinely don't remember, he lived with his sister and her child. He was there for about eight years until he moved in with me."

"How old was the child?"

"Eight, he moved in when the child was born. His sister was not married and I got the feeling that it was his child, he adored her."

Stewart was thinking that Angel's life got more complicated every time she spoke. He decided that she was not going to be any further help so he would see how she reacted to telling her that they had been in the garage. He slowly withdrew the diary from his pocket she froze when she saw it and opened her mouth to speak and changed her mind.

"Will this help?"

"The address isn't in there, but her telephone number is in the front."

Stewart opened the front cover and there was a mobile telephone number written inside.

Coltrane called his secretary and asked her to look up any McPherson's in the Seattle area. And then he dialled the number inside the notebook cover.

"Let's see if she is still there."

The number rang and was immediately cut off and he disconnected the call and his phone rang, it was his secretary.

"There is only one McPherson in the Seattle area, it's not a common name, she gave him the address."

"Organise a visit to the address tell them to detain any males there, nobody is to leave."

She was trying to speak to him.

"Another call has just come in, its Agent Townsend, he's one of the men you left guarding the trailer park."

"Put him on"

Townsend sounded exited.

"Sir, the garage just burst into flames, it's a terrific fire. I've called the fire service, but I don't think they will be able to save it."

Out of the corner of his eye Coltrane could see that Angel was smiling.

"Very clever, the number I dialled set off a device in the garage."

She was laughing.

"Pity I was about to let your parents go."

He produced some papers from his case.

"These show that your father was in contact with a foreign government, he's a traitor. Nobody will let him go; you will all spend the rest of your lives in jail."

She leaned forward and hissed.

"I don't think so unless you are prepared to sacrifice the FBI and CIA buildings and the Supreme Court. You need to let them go now."

Coltrane reacted quickly by grabbing her hands and fixing handcuffs. There were several agents in the corridor, and he pushed her out to them.

"Put her and her parents in a plain panel van; do it quickly, they are not to have any contact with anybody. Bring the van out to the front entrance, we'll join you and tell you where to take them."

Angel was listening to his instructions.

"That won't help you, when Ted finds out that we are not here he will destroy this building."

Stewart had the reply that Angel did not want to hear.

"His first target is you and your parents; he will want you dead before you can provide us with what we need to know. We are your best chance of survival if we take you to a place where he can't find you."

The panel van was out front of the building with two SUV's in attendance. Coltrane ran back to them and explained he did not want them to leave with the panel van.

"Two of you are to get into the back of the van and tell the driver to follow us."

He joined Stewart and they got into their car and gave the driver the first address. It was a detached house on a small housing estate, as they drove onto the driveway a man came around the building and stood in front of the vehicles. Stewart could see that he was armed and the way he stood showed that would handle any trouble. Coltrane spoke to him and they shook hands. Stewart went with Coltrane and Angel into the house and they went to the first floor which had been modified so that it was a self-contained apartment. The door at the top of the stairs was strengthened and the windows were barred on the inside. Coltrane removed Angel's handcuffs and pushed her through the door before it was slammed and locked. Without saying anything to Angel they retraced their steps to the hallway below where they were joined by a young female agent.

"Stewart will you ask the two of the guards in the van to join us here."

When they arrived, he explained that they were staying here with the man and the woman who was his wife to secure Angel.

Without any further explanation he walked out to the van and Stewart followed him.

"Four agents to guard a single woman, are you expecting trouble?"

"We weren't followed from the CIA building, but I am hoping that McPherson will find us."

They all drove to an industrial estate and entered a concrete factory type building. Inside it was converted to individual cells that house inmates who shouted when they heard footsteps.

"What is this place?"

"It's a detention block for undesirables, mostly here without a trial. They are identified by a number and they do not talk to each other. Angel's parents will each have a cell, I would like to leave them for a week before talking to them, but we cannot waste time. They'll be on their own for a couple of days while we take a holiday in Seattle." He was of course referring to a visit to McPherson's sister's address.

Chapter twenty-three.

Coltrane and Stewart left early on the five-hour flight and Stewart was asleep by the time the aircraft levelled off. He missed breakfast but woke for lunch and decided that the rest was what he needed.

"Hello, have you woken up, great company you are." He was grinning so Stewart assumed he must have slept also.

They were collected by another three security men organised by the NSA and after the usual checks set off to drive to McPherson's sister house. On the way Coltrane checked in with the office who advised them that there were agents watching the house they were expected and that there had only been one visitor and he was still inside; they would detain him if he tried to leave. They described him as middle aged and clean shaven. The door was opened by McPherson's sister who seemed surprised to see them. She obviously had not noticed the agents sitting in a car further down the road; they had changed at regular intervals. Also, if she was in contact with her brother, she must have considered a visit by the CIA was possible. She invited them in and offered them coffee before asking their business which was strange.

"How can I help you?"

"Can you tell us where we might find your brother?"

"No idea, I only see him a few times a year."

"When was the last occasion?"

"Not sure, month ago perhaps."

Coltrane produced the photographs of Chapman and McPherson.

"Do you recognise either of these two men?"

She studied Alan Chapman's image and handed the photograph back.

"Never seen that one."

She studied the other photograph for an even longer time.

"This one is like my brother but it's not him. Anyway, Ted has a beard, when was it taken?"

"Some time ago."

"It's not him."

You have a man staying here, can we see him?

"He's asleep."

"Wake him up."

"Only if you tell me why you want to talk to him."

Coltrane moved to the doorway.

"Call him or I will go and wake him."

"OK don't get excited."

She called up the stairs and the man appeared immediately, he was fully dressed and had obviously been listening to their conversation from the top of the stairs. He was a close match for the two men in the photographs.

"You are?"

"Giles Langford."

"Driving licence, identity card or passport please."

"I don't have a passport, never needed one and my driving licence is in my car. It's in a garage being repaired."

"Where is that?"

"Other side of town, I used a taxi to get here."

Stewart knew that a high proportion of US citizens did not have a passport. He was studying the man closely. Was this the man he had known at Boeing, but he could not make his mind up.

"What do you do?"

"I'm unemployed but I used to work in a computer store, they closed down."

Stewart asked a few more questions hoping the man would slip up and give a wrong answer, but he did not, he was careful.

"Why are you asking all these questions, I've not done anything wrong?"

"I think you are Ted McPherson, Janet's brother."

"I'm not Ted, I know she has a brother, but I've never met him."

Coltrane stepped right up to him and stared at his face.

"You are the man in that photograph who we are reliably informed had a beard. You have a ruddy complexion and a white chin. You have shaved your beard off in the last few days."

He did not flinch but Stewart detected a small change in his eyes. They had him.

"I shave every day with a wet razor so my chin will be white."

"Not so."

Coltrane stepped behind McPherson; he produced some handcuffs and clipped them on McPherson. He signalled with his head towards the door and Stewart moved quickly down the hall and called the agents from the car. While this was going on McPhersons sister produced a handgun from inside her coat and was trying to aim it. It was obvious that she was not used to weapons and was having trouble levelling it. Coltrane reacted by throwing her brother against her and they both fell. The gun went off and there was silence as every one of them tried to find out where the bullet had gone. It was in the wall and nobody was injured.

"Everybody alright?" One of the agents asked the question.

Coltrane, as usual was the first to react.

"Cuff that one and take them in, we'll talk to them at the office."

The agents took them to their car and Stewart walked down with them; Coltrane called for their car to be brought down from the end of the road as a small campervan drew alongside. One of the agents explained.

"This is our backup unit, it was in a side street so I called it over, we may need more people." There were two agents with the backup unit; they had probably been using it during surveillance changeovers. Stewart could tell that Coltrane was relieved to see the extra agents.

"We'll follow behind you; leave two agents and the backup unit here to keep watch on the house. We'll return later to search it."

The agent's car with two agents and Ted and his sister set off and Coltrane and Stewart followed a short distance behind.

"Some progress at last we have McPherson, his sister and Angel and her parents, OK we lost the garage, but we are definitely further forward."

Coltrane grinned. "We will get something out of that lot."

The deafening noise took them by surprise, ahead of them the other car had collided with a pick-up. There was a large cloud of dust and it looked as though the agent's car would turn over. Very quickly two more cars appeared from which armed men were alighting. The driver of Coltrane's car reacted very quickly but could not stop the car in time before it slammed into the car in front. Realising that this was a staged incident he opened the doors and told Stewart and Coltrane to get out and take cover. Fortunately, Coltrane had the handgun which he had taken from Janet McPherson. Almost immediately firing started and bullet holes appeared in both open doors. If they had not got on the ground as quickly as they did there would have been bullet holes in them. By keeping flat they could see what was happening, Coltrane emptied the handgun in the direction of the assailants. The McPherson's were not treating it like a rescue in fact Ted was struggling with one of the assailants who was dragging him towards one of the cars. His sister was attempting to help him, she was screaming and one of the assailants turned her around and put his handgun to her forehead. Stewart assumed for a second that it was a threat to tell her to stop. The back of her head erupted, and a second shot sounded, it was an execution.

The assailants were silent, they were not shouting, and their actions were calm and deliberate. It was a well-planned operation to abduct McPherson. A single voice called out some instruction, possibly telling them to leave; it was a foreign language which they agreed later that they had not recognised. As quickly as they had arrived the assailants departed leaving four casualties, one injured agent, one dead agent, one dead assailant and Janet McPherson also dead. Neither Coltrane nor Stewart was hurt and they stood up as two police cars screamed to a halt. The police officers were out of their cars in a flash, guns at the ready. There was a brief delay while they explained themselves before the incident was called into headquarters and a search started. Neither of them could state the make and colour of the vehicles but the police seemed to expect them to know the registration numbers. Stewart stood with Coltrane looking down at the dead assailant.

"He's an Arab."

"I can't be certain, but I think they were all Arabs."

"And that voice could have been Arabic."

Coltrane leant against one of the police cars, his voice trembled.

"We had him, and we lost him. It will be hard to find him again."

Stewart could only agree.

"Very."

Luckily, their driver and the other agent in the car were not injured and the car was serviceable, so they decided to go back and search the house, they were not hopeful of the Police department catching the assailants. The house was very untidy and there were indications that other people slept there so Coltrane arranged that the local CIA agents would continue to watch the place.

"We can't be in two places at once so I think we would be better off back in Washington."

Their search did not reveal anything of importance, but they took a computer, a laptop and every letter or document that they could find with them. They caught a late afternoon flight back to Washington. DC. When they got back to the office there were messages for them from the Seattle Police Department and from the CIA in Seattle. The two cars that the assailants had used to make their escape had been found abandoned less than a mile away. The local CIA office had nothing to report; they did not appear to be aware of the possibility that the assailants were Arabs. Coltrane handed the computer and laptop over to the technicians for analysis, while Stewart sorted through the letters and other papers. It soon became clear that he was wasting his time, it was all domestic stuff. He looked for hidden meaning in the letters but found none. Meanwhile Coltrane had gone to meet the technicians who were examining the computer and laptop. They had broken into them quickly and were studying the files.

"The McPhersons seemed to have links with many antinuclear organisations, but it was just talk. We have not found any references to taking control of the remote hijack software. Janet McPherson was in contact with several protest groups, women's rights and things like that, nuisances but not dangerous."

"Any connections to overseas groups?"

"Nothing like that."

They promised to carry on studying the files and would report back if they found anything. Coltrane returned to his office where Stewart had been working on the papers they had found.

"Anything?"

"Nothing, it's surprising they were either not involved, or they have been very careful."

Chapter Twenty-four.

Washington D.C.

Coltrane decided to start the questioning with Angel who was visibly upset at still being in the cells. They decided not to tell her that Ted McPherson had been abducted.

"Are you letting my parents go, they haven't done anything wrong."

"Except for discussing nuclear disarmament with a foreign government which is treason."

"They weren't discussing disarmament; it was just talk. Every country has people who talk about it, but nothing is ever done."

"We need to talk to McPherson, where is he?"

"No idea."

"We'll have to talk to your father and mother, perhaps they can help."

"I've already told you my mother is not very well please leave her alone."

"We'll see."

They moved on to her father who was equally upset that his wife was being held for interrogation.

"I personally don't know anything about this matter, but my wife knows even less. I am happy to discuss it with you provided you release her first."

Coltrane moved in front of him.

"I make the rules here and your wife will stay until I am ready to release her. If you decide not to provide the information that we need you, your wife and your daughter will stay here until you do."

They watched him slump slightly in his chair. He was elderly looking with white hair and a beard. They had read his history, he had served in the navy, seeing service in Vietnam as a deck officer.

"Tell me about your navy time."

He sat up slightly.

"They were good times; the United States Navy was respected then."

"It still is. We're you involved with nuclear weapons?"

"No, conventional weapons were sufficient."

"But you don't like nuclear weapons."

"Of course, I don't. No reasonable person does."

"Is that why you joined the nuclear disarmament movement. Before you answer we have been in the garage that is across the road from your trailer. You were communicating with people of a similar mind in Iran."

They saw an immediate change, he focused on Coltrane and in a much deeper voice.

"Apparently your generation is not bothered, but there are countries like Iran and North Korea that will take advantage of the situation. We have to curtail their efforts now."

"Were you in contact with North Korea?"

"You can't talk to those bastards. But there are people in Iran who, like us want to see all nuclear weapons destroyed and we may have just achieved that, we are managing what governments have not been able to do. I am proud of that. It hasn't actually happened yet, but I hope it does."

His head was held high.

"What can you tell us about Iran?"

"Crap country, full of ambition but not able to do anything about it."

"They've taken control of the software that can remotely control aircraft."

That stopped him, he was visibly shocked.

"They've what, I don't believe you."

"It's true, they captured Ted McPherson. You remember him, he is married to your daughter."

"He lived with her as Alan Chapman who had died, they never married. As for those Iranians they are crazy and dangerous."

He went quiet for a minute while he was thinking.

"This puts us, the three of us in an incredibly dangerous position. Now that they have got what they want they will have no further use for us. If you release us, we could be killed."

"Why would they do that?"

"Because we were working with some people from the Iranian Embassy who would not want to be identified."

"So, tell us who they are, and they will have no reason to harm you."

"You have to keep us in a safe place, then and only then will I identify the Iranians."

Stewart had not spoken during this exchange

"You were obviously working with the Iranians; it was not just linking up with an Iranian protest movement."

"The Iranians are government officials; you do realise that there isn't an Iranian Embassy here. You have to deal with something called the Interests Section which is deniable if they agree to anything."

"Whatever." Coltrane and Stewart left him and returned to Angel's cell.

"Are they all right?" she asked quickly.

"Perfectly."

"So, will you let them go?"

"Not yet we don't believe the names your father gave us at the Iranian Interest Section."

"You mean Jason Baghi and Isa Amiri, they worked with us to take you hostage."

She was pointing at Stewart, her attitude annoyed him.

"You are worried because we are not letting you go free but if you had captured me, I doubt if you would have released me."

"Not our problem, you would have disappeared into Iran or some other place over there."

Coltrane seemed to be aware of the current situation regarding Iran.

"You are very naïve, Iran is committed to pushing Israel into the sea, but Israel has nuclear weapons and they haven't. For a long time, they have tried to develop or acquire them because then they can face off Israel with a conventional war. Now their problem will be solved in a different way, when Israel has decommissioned its nuclear weapons, Iran can start a war with conventional weapons. You are guaranteeing a war in the Middle East."

"But not a nuclear war."

"People will still die."

"Not my problem."

"I take it that you understand that the same situation exists in other parts of the world, we will see wars were, for example, North Korea attacks South Korea or China attacks Japan."

She was shaking her head; she did not seem to care.

Coltrane had clearly come to a decision and arranged for the three of them to be detained until further notice. During the drive back to the office they were both noticeably quiet, they were lost in their own thoughts. They settled down in Coltrane's office and he summed up the situation.

"We have not progressed, we have three people that are part of Global Action who can't tell us anything else that can help us, we now know the identity of two Iranians who we won't be able to talk to and we suspect that they have McPherson. The Iranians control several terrorist groups, so those terrorists have the remote-control system at their disposal, the situation could not be any worse."

Stewart stood up and headed for the door.

"There is nothing that we can do, I think I'll take a break and have a few days off work, I have a funeral to attend and many meetings arranged to sort out my brother's affairs."

"Wait a moment we have to do something."

"We have nothing to go on. You must find McPherson, but we do not know if he is here or somewhere abroad and we suspect that Iran is involved but cannot be sure. We must wait for them to make the next move. We don't even know who they are, it's not Global Action anymore."

Before Coltrane could answer he was through the door.

Chapter Twenty-five.

Syria several years earlier.

The overpowering heat finally woke Emir, and he struggled to stand up. The rush mat that was used as a door was tied back and hung limply, there was not a breath of wind.

He glanced around and checked to see if any other members of his family were still asleep. They had all gone, he was alone. His father usually got up early so that he could work in the field before it got too hot. He was not sure where his sister and mother would have gone, possibly to fetch water. Their one room shack was made of corrugated iron sheets, rusted corrugated iron sheets, when he touched one of them it burnt his fingers. He was not checking to see if it was hot but to gauge the time, he estimated that it was still early morning. He stumbled though the doorway and the sun hit him like a furnace. There was one tree nearby and when he got near to it he could feel the benefit of its shade. He had washed the day before and was not planning to have one now, but the thought of cold water was tempting. The water containers were missing so his mother and sister had probably gone to fetch some water from the spring. Once he had tasted nice clean water when a traveller had stopped to ask the way and given him a clean bottleful. Their spring water was brackish and faintly brown, it tasted awful compared to that which the traveller had given him.

He knew he was in Syria which was the best country in the world but he had never been away from where he lived. Once, with his father they had walked to the low hills at the edge of the plain and looked back at their shack, it was one of several that were in a cluster around the spring. He remembered that day when he had experienced fear and wonder. The fear was because their shack represented safety and he did not like to be too far away from it. The wonder was because he was close to the hills that were on the edge of the plain and he wanted to know what was on the other side of them.

He leant back against the tree and considered his situation; he was not sure about his full name, everybody called him Emir, or how old he was, but he was definitely older than his sister. Neither of them had been to school nor had they travelled anywhere. Their parents scratched a living from their land, they grew enough crops to feed them and they sold some to their neighbours, one of them had two donkeys and he took some of their produce to market. When he returned, he had various goods that his parents had ordered. That neighbour had told him about the outside world which sounded amazing, but even he had only been as far as the village on the other side of the hills and warned him about the evil that was there. His father and mother believed that they were lucky as they had all that they needed.

Some years before a war had started in Syria but it did not reach them. They often saw aircraft flying high overhead, they heard explosions and saw columns of black smoke, but it was always some way off. His parents never talked about it because it did not affect them. Now as he sat under the tree he was thinking if there was more to life. He made a quick decision, he went into the shack and searched for a water container. He found a small one that was half full and without another thought he set off for the hills. He had to choose his way very carefully because somebody would see him as he crossed the flat plain but there were shallow gulley's and he used them. When he had to go onto the flat ground, he checked carefully that nobody was in sight, he looked carefully for his parents and his sister, he never saw them. He did not know on that day that he would never see them again. He crossed the hills which were not as high as he thought they would be, as he crossed the top he resisted the urge to look back, that would have been like saying goodbye but part of him knew he had already said goodbye. The slope downwards on the other side was gentler than the climb that he had just come up. The village was in sight and it was bigger than he had expected, as he got nearer, he could see a lot of people. The mosque was the central building which he intended to visit as there was not one or even a holy man near their shack. There were traders and donkeys everywhere, he even had to move out of the way as a motorcycle went past. It was all new to him, so he walked everywhere, taking it all in. Eventually he felt so tired that he sat down and leaned his back against a wall and drank some of his water. He was trying to work out what he was going to do next, he was wearing the only clothes that he possessed, and he had no money. He must have dozed because he had not noticed the man who was standing in front of him.

"I've not seen you before."

He was dressed in dark clothes and it took a minute or two before he realised that the stranger was a holy man. He felt he had to be careful because he might be in the wrong place or even in trouble.

"I'm sorry sir, this is my first visit and I don't know what to do."

"Where are you from?"

Emir waved a hand back in the general direction that he had walked.

"Half a day over there." He was unsure of himself; would they send him back.

"Are you hungry?" Emir could only nod.

"Come with me." He got up and went with the man who led him to the mosque. He could only stare at the huge building that was made from stone. The man removed his shoes and placed them with some others, as he did not have any shoes, he just followed him through the main hall into a kitchen area at the rear. There were four people working there and they all greeted him as though they knew him, they were cooking food. It smelt delicious but he was led past it into an area that was all white, one of the women indicated that he should was his hands. Then they led him back to where they were cooking and sat him at a table next to the holy man who was already eating. Food and water appeared, and he made himself eat slowly, at home he would have sat on the ground and eaten quickly.

 The holy man did not speak until they both finished eating.

"Tell me about yourself, are you alone?"

He told him everything about himself.

"So, you have nobody with you, you have nowhere to stay and you have no money."

Emir could only nod.

"We will help you. For now, you can stay here at the mosque."

"I am willing to work."

"You can help in the kitchen and with the cleaning."

That night they gave him a blanket and he slept on the ground in a large room with some other people. It was no difference to sleeping at the shack, but somehow, he felt different. This arrangement went on for a long time, probably months during which time he learned the ways of the village and made a lot of friends. He was even offered work by a local trader who would pay him and provide accommodation in his loft over his business. He declined and thanked the man who asked the question.

"What do you intend to do with yourself, are you going to serve Allah."

Emir knew he could not do that because he did not read or write. A man in the store who had listened to their conversation moved closer and spoke quietly.

"You would do well to accept his offer, he is a good man and he has three daughters, he needs a son."

Emir knew what he was hinting at but not being able to read and write was still a problem. That night in bed he thought about it, he needed some schooling and until he got that then the mosque was a comfortable place. He resolved to speak to the holy man at the next opportunity.

He awoke next morning to the sound of truck engines. He had only ever seen one truck which occasionally passed their shack, it was always the same truck. It was obviously incredibly old, rusty and in poor condition, he had no idea where it was going, and it did not come back. He assumed it was on a circular route. The trucks stopped outside the mosque and when he went outside, they were in a line that stretched back to the other side of the village. He had never imagined that there were so many trucks. There was writing on the side of the trucks which were packed with soldiers. "Who do they belong to?" One of the watchers answered.

"They're ours, the Syrian Army." He felt reassured.

The soldiers had climbed down and were taking food from the shops and market stalls and throwing it onto the back of the trucks. The watching crowd was growing restless but backed away when rifles were aimed at them. The drivers of some of the trucks started blowing their horns and the soldiers climbed aboard and the trucks started moving. As they passed by Emir saw that some were towing trailers with large guns. As the dust died down, he saw the holy man in excited conversation with some of the villagers, he walked up to listen.

"They are retreating, that's what they are doing."

"And taking most of our food with them." He could see that the shops had been emptied.

"At least they moved out quickly, if the rebels are chasing them, we wouldn't want them to meet here."

The tidying up began as they heard more engines in the distance. This time it was the rebels who arrived in a ragged column, unlike the Syrian Army their vehicles were a selection from anything they could find. Most of them were pickups which had been modified to carry heavy machine guns and some even carried anti-tank weapons. If the vehicles looked in poor condition the soldiers looked worse, they were clothed in a wide variety of civilian clothes which meant they did not look like a fighting force. Even Emir realised what they were, he had seen the faces of the Syrian Army soldiers who were fleeing from them and looked frightened. They arrived in the village and just like the Syrian Army before them they started to loot the shops, except the Army had already taken most of the food and there was little left. Emir understood what was happening, the Syrian Army had taken almost everything so that the following rebels would struggle to find food. The Army while appearing to be fierce had not abused any of the villagers but the rebels were different, any men that appeared fit enough to fight were given the choice of joining the rebels and if they refused were soundly beaten. They also turned their attention to the women, even entering houses to find them, screams rang out as many were raped. This was something that Emir had never seen before and he realised there was nothing he could do to help.

There was so much noise that they never heard the aircraft until they were almost overhead. They attacked the convoy by starting from the front which effectively blocked the way out of the village. Then they attacked the rear which effectively bottled up the whole village. The rebels manned their machine guns and one aircraft was hit. Some of the aircraft carried bombs and systematically dropped them on the rebel vehicles whose occupants fled for cover in the nearest buildings. A second wave of aircraft included some helicopters who were carrying barrel bombs, they were intended to kill people even those in a building. They were large oil drums that were full of explosive and were dropped from a low height with great accuracy. The helicopters returned time after time and were systematically destroying the village and the rebels.

Emir fled into the hardware store which he knew had a basement and he descended the steps to find it full of villagers. As the bombs exploded the cellar filled with dust and part of the roof fell in trapping some people but nobody was killed. There was sporadic firing for some time after the sound of the last aircraft died away, and the rebels and villagers emerged from the rubble. As Emir went into the main street, he could hear somebody explaining why the Syrian Airforce had bombed its own people. Apparently, they always tried to attack the rebels in a village or town where they were hemmed in. If they tried to attack them in open countryside the rebels simply scattered. There were bodies and injured villagers everywhere and the village was almost totally destroyed. The surviving rebels were trying to find working vehicles that could be used to escape. One of them grabbed him by the arm and took him to a half buried pick up which had very little damage and set him to work to help dig it out. They were expecting a land attack and the Syrian Army convoy that had gone through earlier could return to finish them off. In a remarkably short time, they had eight working vehicles which were covered with rebels ready to leave. The rebel who had put him to work came up to him.

"Are you coming with us?"

Emir shook his head.

"Please yourself if you stay you will die here. When the government forces get here, they will kill everybody."

Emir thought quickly and climbed onto the back of a pickup as it drove away, he knew he was joining the rebels. Instead of following the track that went through the village the escaping rebels drove across country. That way they would not be caught up by the Syrian Army columns. As there was no marked track their progress was slow and it was a whole day later before they entered a large town, this was one of their strongholds as they were greeted rapturously. Emir saw the sign as they entered the town, he had to do something about his reading and writing. He was immediately accepted as a rebel and he found some clothes and a weapon. As he did not have any knowledge about guns, he had no idea what it was, but it gave him the feeling that he was part of what was happening. Later he wandered into a huge marquee were everybody was eating; he joined a queue for food and was surprised when nobody asked him for money. There was a space at a table, so he sat next to a young woman who smiled at him.

"Is all the food free?"

"Everything and at night you find an empty bunk to sleep, it's not your bunk, if you return the next night there will be somebody else using it. Have you just arrived?"

"Yes."

"Where from?"

"Don't know, I just climbed on a truck which came here."

"Well this is Kherbet Alsoda which is west of Homs and we control this town, the army occasionally attack us but don't attempt to drive us out. It suits them to know where we are."

"What did you do before you joined us."

"Worked on my father's land, I need to learn to read and write but I suppose that is out of the question now."

"I will teach you; I was a teacher and taught infants. It often takes two months but will take four here."

"Why longer?"

"You will find out; they will expect you to do duties."

"Sounds right."

"There is a price that you have to pay me."

"I don't have any money." She laughed.

"I don't want money; I want you to stay by my side all the time."

Emir was puzzled.

"If I walk about alone, I will be sexually assaulted, if I point my gun in their face it makes them keener. The best solution is to have a man with me."

Emir could not believe his luck; he would be taught to read and write and have the company of a young woman thrown in.

"Don't get any ideas, I just teach you to read and write."

He smiled; they would have to see how it worked out.

"I'm Rula what's your name?"

"Everybody calls me Emir, but my full name is Juda Emir,"

She did not laugh so he had got his name right, at least it must have sounded Syrian.

Chapter Twenty-six.

Washington.

It was the day that Stewart had been dreading, his father's funeral had been stressful, but he expected his brother's to be worse. Deep down he blamed himself for Alistair's death, if he had not moved to Washington it would not have happened. Worse still he felt that he should not have agreed to Alistair taking his place. He did not know any of Alistair's friends from New York or any of the people he had worked with, which meant he could not let them know about Alistair's death. He placed notices in the obituary columns of all the New York papers and waited for the flood of contacts, which never happened. Even his previous girlfriend who Stewart had met did not make contact.

He was the only beneficiary of Alistair's will and found it was more substantial than he had thought it would be. There was a substantial property portfolio which included apartments and office space in both New York and Washington, fortunately they were managed by an agent who would continue to handle them. Investments and tax were dealt with by a prominent firm of Washington accountants which meant that he could leave that arrangement in place. His only problem was Alistair Phillips Incorporated, the company based in the offices below the apartment where he lived. He could not run that company himself nor did he wish to. As it had a good management team he decided to leave it as it was until he had time to think about. Several competitors had expressed interest and a management buyout had been suggested. The funeral itself went very well with many business and government departments sending representatives who he did not know as he had never been involved in Alistair's work. One thing was immediately obvious, he would never need to work again but was glad of this time away from the situation that was going on around him due to his involvement with the military and the CIA.

At first he found he was enjoying the break even though he was still under close guard and had a resident security officer in the apartment. He was waiting for the news of an aircraft crashing into a building and when this did not happen, he settled down to a routine of working from home. Fourteen days after walking out of Coltrane's office he was enjoying the breakfast that Rosie had just made when the phone rang, it was Coltrane.

"OK, I hope you have had time to sort out all those personal matters. Time to get down here and deal with the worsening situation. I've had three calls this morning that we have to deal with."

"Who from?"

"Just get down here."

Coltrane was obviously rattled about something, so he finished his coffee and advised his security detail that he was leaving for the office. Darren immediately went down to the carpark to check the car and Rosie and Aaron collected their things and were ready to leave with him. He suspected that they were relieved at the prospect of doing something other than hanging around while he attended to Alistair's estate.

Coltrane appeared calm when he entered his office, so much so that he suspected that he had fallen for a ruse that was designed to get him back to the office.

"What do we have to deal with?"

"Bennett was on the phone earlier, has a couple of problems that he needs our help with."

"He needs our help, I thought he was in control of the situation.?"

"So, did I but since our meeting with Fisher at Dulles Airport the opposition have taken Fishers wife and children hostage."

"Bennet never told us."

"I think he was too embarrassed to admit he had not kept them secure and hoped he would sort it out quickly. Also he probably felt it was more to do with his operation than ours."

"How does this affect us?"

"There's more, it gets worse. They, the Arabs, got a message to Fisher that they had his family and Fisher promptly absconded."

"Absconded, as in escaped. Bennet had him under arrest for goodness sake."

Stewart held his hand up to indicate that he was thinking.

"This gets more complicated by the minute. They have McPherson who we are assuming changed the entry protocols of the software but does not know how to use it. That explains why they have not used the remote-control system during the last two weeks. Also this explains why they have taken Fisher's family hostage; they needed him again to show McPherson again to use the software.

"Why would that be?" Coltrane asked.

"Because he accidently or deliberately gave them some wrong information".

"You'll need to explain that to me."

"When entering information in about the aircraft that you are hijacking or going to take control of you have to enter certain information in a specific sequence, get it wrong and the program shuts down and has to be re-booted. Fisher carried out those take overs in North Korea while McPherson watched and that would satisfy them that the system worked and it's only now that they realise that Fisher tricked them."

"Got it, Bennett needs our help to find Fisher before he can be forced to help them again, and Fisher needs our help to make the software safe so it can't be used."

"Which we can't do until we get our hands-on McPherson so that he can tell us how to get past the security that he has changed."

It was a hopeless situation.

"You said there was three messages, what was the other?"

"Better news, the Arab that was killed during the ambush in Seattle was a Syrian."

"How did they find that out?"

"He had nothing on him, no papers to identify him but he had a tattoo which identified him as a member of the Taliban."

"Stupid thing to do."

"The coroner found it, a tiny one under his left armpit, very easy to miss apparently."

"How does that help us?"

"He was one of a small group who entered the country legally and we have been watching them since their arrival. They have apparently behaved themselves, but they are here for a purpose."

"Where can we find them?"

"They are based in Baltimore."

"Baltimore."

"There's an echo in this room."

"How many are there?"

"Nine who are constantly watched. I have issued instructions that no action is to be taken until we decide."

"Time to visit Baltimore again and the first thing that we need to do is have another talk with Angel and her parents."

Chapter Twenty-seven.

Baltimore.

Angel had not been told that they were about to talk to her, so much so that when they entered her cell, she did not bother to turn around to see who it was. Coltrane changed that.

"Mrs Angelica Chapman we are here to charge you with terrorist charges."

She turned quickly, either because she recognised his voice or because of the threat.

"What do you mean, I haven't been involved with terrorists?"

Coltrane ignored her outburst and told her what her rights were. She sat down slowly on the edge of the bunk.

"What about my parents?"

"Same charge."

He explained that while she had led them to believe that the family had been talking to Iranian protesters and not the Iranian government they had been dealing with the Taliban. That is a terrorist organisation that is funded and supported by the Iranian government.

"I know who the Taliban are but not personally."

"Well the people you were dealing with are actually Syrians and are members of Qasad a terrorist group who are funded by us, the USA. They support the rebels in Syria who are fighting the government forces who are supported by Russia. You have got yourselves involved with some big players."

She had her head down and mumbled something but did not repeat it.

"They have a presence here and by here, I mean Baltimore. I find it interesting that they are based here, and you and your parents live here. Can you explain that?"

"I know nothing about them, it must be a co-incidence that they chose this city."

"They fly into America and just happen to choose the place where you live, remarkable."

She stayed quiet.

"They've taken Ted McPherson prisoner." She shrugged but did not answer.

"There is a big difference between Global Action calling the shots and an Arab terrorist group who have a full agenda of reforms. We'll see what your parents have to say about this."

Coltrane arranged for both her parents to be put into the same interview room.

"You've decided to interview them together?" Stewart was surprised.

"Husbands and wives often interrupt each other, and I don't think Mrs Krasinski will have much to say and may end up in tears which could affect her husband's attitude."

"You're an unfeeling sod do you know that?"

"Yeh, you could be right, but we need answers.

They were both sitting at a table when they entered the interview room. Coltrane walked in without speaking and sat facing them.

"Crunch time, we've charged your daughter with terrorism. She was dealing with a Syrian terrorist group who have a base here in Baltimore. We will be charging you both with the same offense."

Abe Krasinski did his best to ignore the threat, but his wife blurted out.

"I told you not to trust them."

"Be quiet, we haven't done anything wrong."

Coltrane smiled.

Abe spoke again, "We haven't, one day the world will realise what we have achieved.

She ignored him.

"If I tell you everything will that help us?"

"I said be quiet."

"We were approached by a young journalist, at least he said he was a journalist, from the Iranian Interest's section. I was not sure that he was a journalist, his name was Bashar al Barazi, we met him on several occasions along with another man called Saeed Nabavi. It was never made clear who they worked for, but they helped us by advising us on the best strategy for getting the nuclear weapons decommissioned."

"When you say you never found out who they worked for, you must have had some idea."

"There were several interested parties including Iran, Iraq, Syria and Lebanon."

"They would all be interested, for different reasons."

Abe interrupted.

"They were actually all terrorist groups and they only had one interest, that was curbing United States influence, the countries she just mentioned supported terrorist groups and they used them to hide their own activities."

It was a breakthrough; they were both talking and had acknowledged that they had connections to terrorist groups. They talked for at least another hour but did not really give much more information of interest.

Later Coltrane and Stewart agreed that Angel, her parents, and McPherson had all been used in a clever way. The real answers lay with all their Arab contacts and it was unlikely that they would get the opportunity to interview them.

They moved to another office to find the agent who was dealing with the Syrians who were living nearby. He was Agent Crowe, a cheerful man with a ready smile and a keen interest in 'his' Syrians.

"I knew they would do something eventually; it was just a case of waiting. So, what have they done?"

"Nothing really except one of them got himself killed but you know about that."

He explained that whatever the reasons when certain foreigners who are of interest enter the country they are kept under surveillance until they show they are behaving themselves.

"How many are you talking about?"

"Oh, hundreds."

"You are watching hundreds."

"Good lord, no. We have a group of Syrians living here so we are informed if any leave or if new ones arrive, but they could go somewhere else, Los Angeles for example, there is another group there."

"Sounds like a massive undertaking."

He nodded emphatically.

"What reasons do they give for coming here?"

"Lots of different ones, with Arabs it is often down to education."

He opened a draw in his desk and took out a folder.

"We were notified last week of two new arrivals who at immigration gave the address here in Baltimore that my Syrians use. They are Emir Juda and Rula Asad, they are both here to study international relations between the US and Syria. They are connected to Qasad which is a rebel organisation that is fighting the Bashar al Assad regime. We support Qasad so we are told to act in a kindly manner to them."

"And do you."

"We treat them like any other aliens until we know differently, these two will require keen attention."

"For what reason?"

"They do not fit the mould like the others, they are both young, he is twenty and she is twenty-two, he is a good-looking young man and she is a good-looking woman. He does not speak any English, she is fluent, she is obviously his interpreter which means we cannot talk to him directly. At a guess I would say that he has some special skills and she makes certain he does not talk about it."

"What type of property are your Syrians living in, rented, owned or what?"

"Old house, eight bedrooms in an area that was once very fashionable but has now faded."

"How many of them now live there?"

"There were nine, but we lost one in the shooting and we have these two new arrivals, which means there are ten."

"With eight bedrooms they must be sharing." Geoff Crowe shrugged he was not interested in their sleeping arrangements.

"What do they do?"

"Four of them wash, cook and clean. Four are tourists and spend their time studying everything and the last two are here for international relationship purposes, whatever that is. They are nominal descriptions they could really be here for other purposes"

"Is the house rented? "

Crowe nodded.

"So their government pays the rent."

"No, we do. "

"Has there been any sign of a non-Arab visiting or staying there in the last two weeks?"

"Not that I am aware of, but I'll have the tapes checked."

"You have them under surveillance?"

"There is a Veterans Club opposite to the house, so we placed a camera there. It downloads via the internet to this building."

Before they left him, they asked him to check if any flights were booked by any of the residents to Seattle in the previous three weeks. Later in the car on the drive back to Washington they agreed that they had got little bits of information which amounted to nothing.

Crowe was one of those agents who dealt with requests in a prompt way, next morning he reported that a man had been helped into the house. He seemed to be either drunk or drugged, he had not been seen leaving so must be in the house. Regarding the flights to Seattle, four Syrians had flown out and only three had flown back on the same weekend as one of them was killed.

"McPherson is there, can we get him." Stewart was certain it was that easy. Coltrane grimaced.

"We can't just march in; it involves another country. I'll have a word with Crowe and a few other people and see what can be done."

It only took a couple of hours to arrange an anti-Syria demonstration outside the house. Ten demonstrators, some with placards would arrive and throw some army thunder flashes at the house, they would break a few windows and force their way into the house. The police would arrive in force to take charge of the situation, they would be CIA with Stewart and Coltrane amongst them. The house would be thoroughly searched for any demonstrators that had broken in. Stewart and Coltrane's job was to identify McPherson if they found him there. Stewart could not believe that the CIA would go to such lengths, it was planned for the next morning.

They had to return to Baltimore so left that night and stayed in a safe house so that they were ready for an early start and were collected by a police van. Inside was a selection of police clothing and riot gear which they changed into as the van was driven to the house. They settled down to wait with the other agent's half expecting to be sent around to the house within a few minutes. It was almost thirty minutes before the engine started and they moved off. A surprising sight greeted them, the road outside the house was almost blocked with cars, a police officer who was a genuine policeman explained.

"Hi guys, we did not know you were on duty, there is a demonstration going on here and a lot of people have turned out to watch, park over there."

He indicated a space further down the road.

"We are parking on the pathway, as close to the house as possible."

"There isn't space."

"Move some of the black and whites."

Stewart sensed that they were about to get an argument, but Coltrane flashed his CIA identity and the cars were moved very quickly. They all got out of the van and Stewart felt he was manoeuvred with Coltrane to the middle of a bunch of agents who entered the house. He had understood that this would be a quick and quiet operation, but he was faced with a smashed front door and several broken windows. There was a lot of shouting and one Asian man was trying to take charge. He was facing an CIA agent who was dressed in police riot gear who was using delaying tactics so that he and Coltrane could get into the ground floor rooms.

"And you are?"

"Saeed Nabavi, I am in charge here and you must move all these men, they are trespassing."

Stewart recognised the name as one that the Krasinski's had mentioned."

"We will move out when we are satisfied that nothing unlawful is occurring here. We will search the house, please move to one side." He did not wait for Nabavi to comply and pushed him out of the way making space for Stewart and Coltrane to get through. As they reached the bottom of the staircase they were intercepted by an agent.

"We've searched all the ground floor and there are only Arabs there."

As he finished speaking there was a shout from the floor above.

"Up here." They were met at the top of the stairs by another agent who directed them to an open door. Inside the room was a man in a dark suit, he was tied to a wooden chair. He was facing a window and Stewart moved around him so that he could see his face. It was not McPherson but the man was grinning.

Stewart stepped back and signalled to Coltrane to check other rooms, at the same time he slipped his hand inside the man's jacket to find his wallet, his identity could be useful. The blow to the back of his head took him by surprise and as he started to slump, he felt powerful hands lift him off the floor. One hand was clasped firmly over his mouth as he vaguely recognised that he was being lifted out of the window and onto a fire escape. He was struggling and desperately trying to clear his head as he was manhandled to the ground and through a gap in the fence and into the adjacent property. The last thing he heard was the door slamming and it went quieter. When he came around, he was tied to a chair and McPherson was similarly restrained next to him.

"Are you OK?"

Stewart nodded; his head was throbbing.

"They were waiting for you; it was a set up. Now they have me, you, and Fisher they do not need anything else. All hell is about to be let loose."

"How do you know that they have Fisher?"

"They told me; they were jubilant."

"Who are they?"

"A terrorist group out of Lebanon, they have some interesting ideas. They intend to use the remote-control software to blackmail governments, some will pay them a tax and others will hire their services for using the software to solve their own problems. Their long-term aim is to create a new country called Middle East which will be so powerful that it will dominate world finances and politics."

"They've told you this?"

"No reason for them to deny it."

"Are we staying here in America?"

"No idea but thinking about it they will move us to somewhere like Iran."

"None of this would have happened if you had not changed the security codes."

McPherson lowered his head and came to a decision.

"Just enter the passwords and codes in reverse order, spell them backwords."

Stewart realised it was a simple solution that nobody had thought of.

"And those two incidents, the Washington one and the North Korean ones, did you do those?"

"No Fisher did that right in front of them, he knew what to do and they did not notice."

"What did you change?"

McPherson smiled.

"I changed the order of the questions, for example when the program asks for the height for the flight of the hijacked aircraft you are actually answering the question for the direction it will fly. The program doesn't accept a heading as a height setting and closes down."

"Simple."

"The simplest ideas are the best."

Stewart realised that McPherson must have been in contact with Fisher. He also felt a little happier now that he knew the details of the security codes and how the program had been modified to prevent even trained operatives using it. All he had to do was escape with that information.

Chapter Twenty-eight.

Washington D.C.

The room was full, extra chairs had been brought in, Coltrane deliberately positioned himself at the far end of the table as far as he could from the President. The meeting had started in a sombre manner but had turned into a noisy argument. The President had brought them to order more than once and had now resorted to a coffee break to calm them down. For several hours, the matter of remote control of aircraft had been discussed from the very start. Coltrane understood that this was because there were some people present who knew little about the situation. There were others who needed updating, he had spent a long time reporting the incident in Baltimore. He was forced to admit that it was sometime before he realised that Stewart was missing. He had explained that he left Stewart in the room with the man who was tied to a chair. When he returned the man had been freed and was standing there and smiling at him, upon closer inspection he looked like was an Arab. He had visited every room in the house and could not find Stewart, yet no one had not seen him leave the house.

The head of Homeland Security asked the question that most of those present felt they already knew the answer to.

"Do you think this was a set-up to capture Stewart Phillips?"

He could only answer.

"Definitely."

"Do you also think that they had help in some way, from official sources?"

"Possibly."

The President intervened.

"Can you elaborate on that?"

"No, I don't have any definite information."

"Are you looking into that?"

"No, we at the CIA have too much to do at present. Our priority is to get those three men back."

The President accepted his reply and summed up the situation.

"These terrorists have now taken some key persons into their custody. They include the only fully trained programmer, an employee of Boeing who was working with the military, they have a partially trained programmer who has altered the entry codes to prevent anyone else gaining access, and they have a CIA operator who is fully trained to use the anti-hijack software. As I understand it none of the three has all the skills to operate the military system, but collectively they can do that. Just as importantly we cannot use the system. Is that a good summary of the current situation?"

There was some muttering around the room, but nobody disagreed, somebody muttered.

"We need to kneel on the floor, put our heads between our knees and pray."

The President effectively brought the meeting to a close.

"We need you all gentlemen to think about how we can resolve this matter urgently, I am assuming that you don't have any positive solutions now."

He stood and as he did so he stared at Coltrane while indicating with his head that he should join him in his office. He was waiting for him at the doorway and refused others who wanted to talk to him from entering the office.

"I need to discuss with you how you think we can resolve this matter. All the others that were in that room can help but the problem is central to you and this fellow Stewart Phillips. Tell me honestly what you think will be the outcome, please don't give me answers for the sake of giving answers."

"Mr. President, they hold all the winning cards and it is up to us to thwart their plans. In the short term we will experience some events using aircraft that will be under remote control and there is nothing we can do about that. Our progress will be down to Stewart Phillips who, whether they like it or not is our agent in their camp. He has to escape to deny them his knowledge."

"Is he capable?"

"I believe so."

"Well, I will leave it to you, but I have to say that my worst fear is that this is the work of a collaboration of different countries. We need to regain total control and quickly!"

He stood and walked out of the room.

Chapter Twenty-nine.

Baltimore.

Stewart was in an upstairs lounge and quickly worked out that it was the house next door to the one that had been raided. Through the windows he could see that the street was clear, obviously all the vehicles that had taken part in the raid had disappeared. He was seated on a wooden chair and when he went to stand up, he found he was fastened to the chair by his ankles with handcuffs. Next to him McPherson was similarly restrained,

"Your hands are free, and you are not gagged, I made a noise and they bound my arms and gagged me. It's better if we keep quiet."

They sat quietly for a while both lost in their own thoughts until the door opened and another chair was brought in, followed by two people carrying Fisher who was unconscious. He was handcuffed to the chair and left to recover. It was a long time before he lifted his head, looked around and saw them, he immediately started shouting for a drink of water. McPherson immediately advised him not to shout and what the consequences would be.

Stewart spoke to him quietly.

"How did they get you?"

"They took my family hostage and told me to meet them, or else."

"Where did you meet them?"

"Dulles Airport."

"I thought you were based at somewhere other than Washington and that you flew in for our meeting."

"The politicians wanted one of the controls near at hand the other is in Montana. That flight, which was not a flight, was a parked-out aircraft that we used."

"I realised that, when we left, I put my hand on one of the engines and it was cold. I still thought you were based somewhere else."

"Do you know where your family is?"

"They say they have released them, but I don't trust them."

"How did you get here?"

"No idea."

McPherson explained

"In the trunk of a car, it backed into the garage at the back of the house, it's connected to the house. They kept you out of sight."

Stewart was looking around the room.

"It isn't safe to talk here." Meaning that they could be recorded, so they sat in silence until they were interrupted by two young Arabs who brought a table and something to eat. The boy who looked younger than the woman only said a few words in Arabic while she spoke good English.

"Everybody alright? "

Nobody answered.

"Cheer up, you are going for a ride tonight."

It was after sunset when they were taken to the garage. They crossed between the two houses and through the fence, the handcuffs on their feet had been removed and used to restrain their arms. They were accompanied by three men and they were gagged. The main garage doors were closed, and they entered through a side door, there were already five men there. A black Ford van was there with its rear doors open; two other cars were parked next to it. They were told to get into the back of the van and were joined by seven Arabs, two of which were the two young ones who had fed them earlier. The rear of the van was closed off by a steel partition which did not allow access to the cab. Two men climbed into the cab the garage door was raised and the engine started, and they moved out into the night air. As they left Baltimore they pulled into a motel and drove alongside another black ford van, its rear doors were open presumably to allow fresh air to circulate. As they stopped, they could hear muted voices which died away as the doors to the second van were closed and it drove away. They left after a few minutes and drove for a long time, many of them dozed but were woken by the young Arab woman.

"We are approaching Dulles Airport and we will remove your gags and handcuffs. You will not mis-behave, or we will stop you." One of the Arabs held up a short club for them to see.

"We will enter an airport building by a side door and you will be taken to a parked aircraft and will be seated. Do not try anything because some of my colleagues here would like to hit you really hard."

When the van stopped, they were next to a fire door that was open. Stewart looked for any opportunity to escape but his captors had the situation under control. They were led down a short corridor and through another fire door which opened directly onto the airfield. Directly in front of them was a large aircraft and they were guided up the stairs into the cabin. The aircraft was sign written in Arabic characters which did not help Stewart to identify it. There were a lot of passengers already on board and they were taken to the far end of the aircraft. As he was seated, he realised that the engines were already running, and that the door had been closed. It felt like an enormous trap had been sprung on him. The aircraft took off and after it had levelled off the young Arab woman explained their situation.

"You are on the way to Iran and you will be pleased to know that I cleared customs control and will clear immigration for you, I used your passports" She held up a bunch of passports for them to see. She must have seen Stewart's puzzled expression because he knew his passport was at home in his apartment. She went on to explain.

"My name is Rula and ten days ago a trade delegation arrived in the US from Iran, despite what you may read the two countries still trade, and they left today. Except this ten people are now that trade delegation and the original is at the house in Baltimore. That is why Emir and I are here; we complete the picture. The original delegation had two young representatives, we are now them and the whole party that is leaving closely imitates the original one that arrived. We left the house in a black van and the delegation arrived in a black van."

 Fisher had not fully understood.

"Why have they gone to that trouble?" he asked Stewart.

"They now have ten operatives in the US without anybody knowing what they look like and we have disappeared. Officially we are still in the country and the trade delegation has left."

"Very clever."

Chapter thirty.

Iran.

Stewart was more concerned with his situation. It's worrying, nobody knows where I am.Stewart was trying to calculate if that gave them an advantage, he would have been happier if he could have got hold of the passport that she had used for him to clear immigration. He was now in a foreign country without a passport, he did not have any contacts, was not sure if the US Embassy was open if he managed to get there.

"Why are we in Iran, you said you and Emir were Syrians."

"We are members of Qasab, an Arab organisation and we are funded by Iran. But that is set to change we will become more powerful and influential than any of the Middle East states. "

When the aircraft landed it taxied to a halt and the door was opened, they were instructed to stay in their seats while the other passengers left the aircraft. When they were told to disembark, they found that the aircraft was guarded by soldiers and there was a small bus waiting for them. They expected to be told where they were being taken but the bus did not leave the airfield. It went to a waiting helicopter which took off as soon as they had boarded. The journey was a short one to another airfield where there were a lot of military aircraft. The three of them were separated from the others and were taken to a prefabricated building which was equipped with beds, chairs, and tables.

"Home sweet home, you get your own accommodation. You start work tomorrow."

With that Rula left the building and locked the door behind her. Stewart checked the windows they were screwed up tight and while doing so saw the guards that were patrolling outside. He wondered where the others were being accommodated, there had been ten of them on the aircraft that left Dulles, all Arabs.

Fisher was the first to speak, he looked worried.

"We are in real trouble."

"Calm down we are OK for now." Stewart tried to reassure him.

"Until they find out that they only need one of us."

Fisher did not know that McPherson had told him how to deal with the program security and wondered if he knew.

"None of us know everything about the program, they need the three of us to operate it."

"You are the only one who knows how the program was written as soon as you are given the security information, they will no longer need McPherson and me."

Stewart was watching McPherson out of the corner of his eye and saw him flinch, he had realised his mistake in confiding with him. Cold food was brought in and not long after that the lights went out, they were prisoners. The beds were piled with loose blankets, so they went to bed. When they were woken by the guards it was already light, and his watch showed eleven o'clock which did not help as he had not reset it after crossing the Atlantic. Stewart, Ted, and Fisher dressed and had a quick wash. The sound of the door unlocking was a good sign until they saw that a squad of armed soldiers were waiting for them.

They were taken to a building at the base of the control tower where they were given a reasonable breakfast of coffee and waffles with honey, they felt better. As soon as they finished, they were taken through a door and up two flights of stairs, on the first floor they passed the control room and on the second they entered a comfortable lounge. It was furnished with comfortable chairs and had coffee making facilities. Along one wall there was a large cupboard that was locked, two windows gave a great view of the airfield. Rula had come upstairs with them and was accompanied by a young armed soldier, in a cheerful voice she announced.

"This is your daytime accommodation if you cooperate and behave yourself you will spend most of your time here, if not you will be in the bedroom for most of the day and all the night. Please relax."

She left the room but the soldier stayed. Fisher was the first to speak again.

"What now?"

"No idea, another cup of coffee perhaps."

"You are too laid back, but of course they don't have your wife and kids, do they."

"Haven't got any of those. It occurs to me that if they wanted to unnerve you then it is working, just calm down, they will tell you what you want to know when they are ready."

Stewart was putting on a calm look but inside his mind was racing. He looked at the soldier.

"Do you speak English?" The man shrugged, thought for a moment before answering.

"A leetle."

It did not matter whether they had a soldier listening in to them or they were recording their conversations, the result was the same. Stewart knew that if he was to get out of this situation, he had to do so himself. The door opened quietly, and a well-dressed army officer entered the room followed by two more armed soldiers.

"Good morning gentlemen, I am Colonel Abrahim Erhaim. We will be working together, hopefully a good relationship."

None of them answered.

"Come gentlemen, we can at least be pleasant even if we don't agree on some matters."

The three of them smiled.

"We are here to use the remote control software that Boeing have created to bring about change in the way world events are controlled, in particular to advance the influence of the Arab nations."

He signalled to one of the soldiers who moved over to the large cupboard and unlocked the doors and folded them back. This revealed a selection of computer equipment.

"That cupboard will be locked when not in use and guarded when you are here, we wouldn't want you breaking the doors and using the internet to communicate with your security services. By the way they have not yet realised that you are out of the country, the USA that is."

McPherson walked over and studied the equipment.

"Only the best."

"We would spend whatever is necessary to achieve our aims. As you can see, we have the right equipment and you will be surprised to know that we have the original software, that was acquired from Boeing with the help of Mr. McPherson."

Stewart and Fisher stared at him, hardly believing what had been said. Stewart now understood what McPherson had been up to when alone in the Boeing office. The Iranian officer continued and ignored McPhersons embarrassment.

"What we do not have is somebody who can use the software properly, I understand that one of you could do that. I have decided that I will shoot two of you, in my own time of course." He signalled to the soldier who lowered his rifle to threaten them.

"If one of you can convince me that you are capable, I will spare him and shoot the other two."

Stewart pointed out. "You could shoot the wrong one and never be able to operate the system."

"You are correct of course so I will start with Mr. Fisher's family in order that you can see that I am serious. We have them in custody."

Fisher responded quickly.

"That's not fair, I can operate the system and know how the security works."

McPherson interrupted.

"No you don't, I had to deal with the security when you did those hijackings to Washington and North Korea. You had no idea how to get into the program. I am the only one with detailed knowledge, I worked on the software at Boeing and changed the security arrangement. I am the one that you need."

The Colonel motioned to the two soldiers who had entered the room with him, they took Fisher by the arms and dragged him down the stairs. The downstairs door slammed shut and a single shot rang out followed by the two soldiers climbing the stairs. When they entered the room they nodded at the Colonel.

Stewart and McPherson sat in silence; the Colonel stared at them.

"So which one of you is going to live?"

McPherson started to bluster.

"You heard what I said, I am the one that you need."

The Colonel motioned to the guards and they took McPherson by the arms and took him down the stairs. Stewart could not understand what had happened but before he could speak the Colonel held up his hand.

"We know that you have more knowledge about the software than anybody else, you worked on it for a long time. We overheard McPherson, while at the Baltimore house, explain the changes to the software to you, we knew you were the one we needed."

"Why did you kill them?"

"It was good fun; they were no longer of any use to us and it tells you that we will not tolerate disobedience."

"And if I decide not to co-operate?"

"More good fun."

The gun shot ended the conversation and they were both silent as the two soldiers came back up the stairs. They came into the room and to the surprise of Stewart one used his rifle to club the soldier who had stayed in the room, the second soldier did the same to the Colonel. The young woman Rula followed them in and four of the Arabs who had been in the house in Baltimore were close behind, they were carrying Fisher and McPherson, both had head wounds and were dead. She went over to the computer cupboard and removed a remote hard drive that was plugged in, it obviously held the software and she closed and locked the cupboard. Then turning she went to the door and checked the stairs were clear before signalling to the soldiers that the Colonel and his soldier should be dealt with, two shots rang out. She turned the lights out and signalled that they should leave the room and she locked the door. They all went down the stairs, outside it was quiet, Stewart would normally have expected somebody from the ground floor to investigate the shots, but nobody did. There were two military vehicles parked behind the building and Stewart was ordered to get inside one along with Rula and two of the Arabs, while one of the soldiers got into the driving seat. The other soldier got into the driving seat of the other vehicle and the other two Arabs climbed into the back. They drove out of the gates and after a few minutes they pulled up outside a rusty industrial building where they parked the military vehicles and all transferred to a bright yellow minibus. It was a long drive before they entered a farmyard and were greeted warmly.

Rula smiled as she stood in front of Stewart who asked.

"What was all that about? I'm grateful that you rescued me but wonder what I am now involved with?"

"Simple, the Iranians solved a lot of our problems, they got you out of the United States and they found out which one of you was important. Without them we would have been faced with the same choices."

"But who are you?"

"We are part of Qasad, they were Iranians and think only of Iran, we have a much wider picture. They wanted the remote-control thing for themselves, we could not let them do that. It is for Arab unity."

"Where will you take me?"

"Northern Iraq we have a secure base there, we will not be interfered with and we have a set-up like the one you saw back there. It is all ready for you to get started. Get some sleep we leave in the morning".

Chapter thirty-one.

Washington.

The President sat back in his chair. And looked directly at Coltrane, "Where is he?"

"We don't know."

"It's your job to know."

"Sir, when we entered that house in Baltimore, he was shoulder to shoulder with me and then he just disappeared."

"You're certain that he did not come out."

"Absolutely certain, we had people outside and a camera watching the house, he did not come out then or since. He must still be in the house; all we can do is keep watching it."

"What about the house next door, somebody suggested he might have gone out that way."

"We checked that house Sir; it's deserted so we broke in one night and it was empty, he was not in there."

"You broke in?"

"Middle of the night, two men in black,"

The President rolled his eyes, he did not want to know any details.

"Could they have taken him out after all the vehicles left?"

"We would have seen that on the camera Sir."

"Find him for goodness sake."

Coltrane and the others nodded

"What about the others, what are they called."

"You mean Fisher and McPherson Sir."

"That's them."

"We don't know where they are either."

The President gave an exasperated sigh and went back to his office.

When he got back to the CIA building, Agents Askin and Lewis were waiting for Coltrane at his own office.

"You two were responsible for Stewart's security, find him now."

"We have nothing to go on. Our country is so big you could lose an army for a year. We have all the ports and airports on watch and we still have nothing. We had an Iranian airliner which came into Dulles and left just after we lost them. The crew and passengers all checked out, there were members of an Iranian delegation on board when it left. Neither Agent Phillips, Fisher or McPherson were seen boarding the plane and were not listed as passengers."

Coltrane just rolled his eyes.

Chapter thirty-two.

Iraq-Syrian border.

Stewart was woken by the young Syrian woman, Rula, she had brought some different clothes for him.

"Get dressed in these, you will blend in, there is coffee downstairs. Don't waste time."

When he got downstairs, he found that a lot of men had arrived, all dressed in military style clothes. Outside were three dust covered four-wheel drive vehicles, he was given a middle seat in the back of one of them, closely hemmed in with no chance of escape. He smiled at his previous optimism, there was absolutely no chance of getting away. They drove out of the farmyard and judging from the position of the sun headed in a north westerly direction. They did not give him any idea as to where they were taking him, and he did not expect them to. They drove for most of the day, passing through some small towns and villages without any incidents. In the late afternoon they approached a border crossing and Rula passed him a passport.

"If they ask for passports give them this one. It is the one that you entered the country with, it is Iranian."

As they reached the guard post a soldier moved alongside and everybody held up their identity documents, so he did the same. The soldier moved away without studying any of them and the barrier across the road went up. Stewart had no way of knowing if that was a tense moment for the others, but it was for him.

"Where are we now?" He was surprised to get an answer.

"We have just crossed into Iraq, it's never a problem. We are close to the borders with Syria and Turkey. If we go into Syria, we will find that the roads are blocked with refugees, thousands of them. We don't go into Turkey"

"Who are they fleeing from?"

"Russians and the Syrian army. We will sort both out shortly."

They drove on until they amongst some hills and turned off the road into a cluster of buildings. The cars stopped in front of a large building that had a welcome committee lined up outside.

Rula got out and stood there with a smile on her face.

"I love this place its beautiful and the air is fresh, the smell of freedom. You are free too, no handcuffs no locks."

He knew what she was saying, he was a prisoner because he did not know where he was, did not speak the language and did not have any papers or transport.

"I'll find you a nice room and introduce you to the people that speak English, there are a few."

The building was a military headquarters but without any external signs, no vehicles or equipment. Despite this he felt certain that it would have been identified from a satellite photograph, it was a small comfort. She took him to a small but basically furnished bedroom, at least it was not a cell. He would have settled for this as a basic holiday home in the countryside, but he knew that the following day was going to be difficult.

"Anything else that you need?"

"Some food, I'm starving."

"After prayers in that building over there." She was pointing to a building that had no walls it was just a roof.

"Alfresco dining."

Her puzzled expression showed that she had not heard the term before. But her reference to prayers reminded him that he was in a Muslim country and a few minutes later heard the Iman calling the faithful to prayer. He did not want to get involved so he went to his room and lay on his bed. He must have fallen asleep because he woke with a start to the noise of people talking loudly, they had finished praying and were queuing at the food hall, he joined them. There was a lot more there than he had expected and he wondered where they had been when he arrived, perhaps there were some underground rooms. As soon as the light started to fade, they disappeared so he went back to his room and could see a lot of them lying on their beds in the open air, there was electricity, but they chose not to use any lights.

He awoke next morning and sat on his bed and listened, there were people quietly moving about so he got up and went in search of breakfast. He took a coffee and a bowl of cereal to a table and sat down; he was joined by a man who spoke good English.

"Your English is good where did you learn it?"

"England, Oxford university. My father was a doctor and I was brought up there."

"Why are you here?"

"I am Syrian, and Syria needs help, so I came here."

"But this isn't Syria."

"No it is too dangerous in Syria but that will change."

Rula was waiting for him when he went back to the main building, she was carrying the hard drive that she had taken from the computer set-up at the airfield. She led the way through the building and to a re-enforced door which opened to a wide flight of stairs going down to a basement. There were several doors and one was guarded by a young Arab who produced a key and opened it. Inside the room was a computer set-up that was similar to the one that he had seen back at the airfield, so much so that he suspected it had been ordered at the same time. Rula went over to it and connected the hard drive so that it was ready for use.

"This is Hadi." She was introducing the young Arab. "He will keep the key to this place and will stay here when you are here, he speaks excellent English as does his replacement. At least one of them will be with you at all times."

"What am I expected to do here?"

"First thing, you will use the system to show the world that we have control of it. Second you will teach Hadi how to use it."

"Is he computer literate?"

"He worked as a computer programmer for Zeonix in the United States, for four years."

Stewart looked at Hadi with renewed respect.

"If I refuse?"

Rula reached into her pocket and produced a crumpled photograph which she handed to him.

"Fishers family. You remember him, we still have them captive in the United States."

She took the photograph back and studied it carefully.

"Pretty aren't they, I can make a mess of them in five minutes."

"And if I decide that those three lives are worth sacrificing to save the world from a bunch of lunatics?"

Rula sighed, he no longer saw her as an attractive young Arab girl.

"Do you remember the trade delegation that has taken your place at the house in Baltimore? Well some of them are part of Qasad and are just waiting to blow some people up in Washington. The explosives are already in place and ready for use, all they need is a couple of days' notice."

She was watching his face and he tried to not show his feelings but had to concede that they had thought of almost everything.

He sat down and switched the computer on, and it started loading the software. Hadi sat beside him watching what he was doing. Rula stopped in the doorway.

"If you are thinking of corrupting the software, forget it, Hadi made a copy last night and I have it in a safe place."

It was another example of their forward thinking; she closed the door quietly. Hadi smiled and offered his hand, Stewart was reluctant to shake it.

"If we are to work together, we might at least be friendly." Then in a quiet voice he said.

"I am in the same position as you, I was working in San Francisco when they took my family hostage and shipped me here."

He did not wait for a reply but dealt with the program. Stewart decided immediately that he might help but he had to be careful, was it possible to trust him? He watched as the familiar program loaded, he had stared at that familiar screen for years at Boeing. Then to his surprise the database of the world's airliners loaded, he had hoped that they would not have access to that information which would have put a temporary stop to their activities.

Hadi looked at Stewart and said, "McPherson told you how to handle the security questions. He said that none had changed but the answers should be spelt backwards."

They had been listening in when McPherson had confided in him. He experienced a flashback to that room in Baltimore when McPherson for some unknown reason decided to help him. He did not hesitate and entered the required answers and the program moved on. He wondered did this mean they knew about the trap that McPherson had set when data was entered? He was about to find out.

Chapter thirty-three.

Stewart decided to explain how the software was used in a logical way which assumed that Hadi had little or no knowledge of computing as it applied to aviation. He soon realised that this was probably not the case.

"There are four steps that once started have to be completed quickly, if you start the set-up, for example, after the aircraft has started to taxi out for take-off and take a long time the aircraft might already be airborne. Similarly if you plan to take control of an aircraft that is approaching an airfield and you take too long it may have landed before you can take control."

Hadi nodded to show he understood.

"Obviously the first decision is to decide which country you wish to target and the second is the actual target itself. You will need the GPS coordinates for that target. Then you must select the airline, you are not targeting the airline itself although they will lose an aircraft. You need the information about the airline to identify the actual aircraft. The next step is to access the airport website and find the departure times, they will also list information about the aircraft that is being used for that flight. The final step at this planning stage is to look that up the aircraft in the database of the worlds aircraft, you have a copy of that database. There are three identifying numbers that are in use. The fin number is displayed on the aircraft, the model number is used by the manufacturer and the actual production number is the one we need. From the manufacturer's records we can obtain the serial number of the autopilot and that is the one that is entered into the program. By continuing to watch the airport website we can monitor the position of the aircraft, whether it is loading, leaving the gate, taxiing, or taking off. By entering the direction that we wish it to fly, the height of the flight and the speed we can take control by just pressing 'enter' on the keyboard. From that moment the aircrew are no longer in control, the transponder, which would report the aircrafts position, is no longer working and all communication is cut. Depending how close to the airfield the target is about five minutes after that the target and the aircraft will cease to exist."

"Wow," was all Hadi could say.

"Have you followed all that?"

"I think so, but you are going to be told to take control of some aircraft."

Stewart hoped Hadi did not know about the trap that McPherson had inserted in the software because he knew he had to use them.

"Where is that to take place?"

"They will be at New York."

"They?"

"One aircraft will take off from La Guardia Airport and crash onto nearby Times Square. Then thirty minutes later, when all the rescue work is underway, two more aircraft will crash at the exact same place."

Stewart paled, this would be wholesale slaughter, Times Square would be packed with tourists.

"You're not serious."

"Not my decision, like you I am doing what I am told. If you decide not to do it a lot of people will die in major cities in the US. Then you will do it."

"Will it have the desired effect?"

"When one aircraft crashes the cause is debateable, when three aircraft from the same airfield crash in the same place it is deliberate. The US government will know they have been sent a message, more importantly every government in the world will understand that message. All of them will listen to what they have to say."

Stewart knew he was going to appear to go through with it, he had no option and he was going to have to trust that McPherson had been telling him the truth.

Hadi had been doing some preparatory work and already knew the GPS co-ordinates for La Guardia airport and Times Square. He had not said so, but he must already have had some knowledge of the software. Stewart was shaking as he started to enter the data into the program that he had worked with for years but never expected that he would ever have to use it, let alone under such circumstances. The airport website provided all the other information that they needed, and they selected three suitable departures with the second thirty minutes behind the first and the third ten minutes behind the second. Very quickly they had the Unalterable Auto Pilot reference numbers and entered the first one into the software which asked the first question which was the height that the hijacked aircraft should follow, this was the point when he had to trust McPherson. If he had been telling the truth the answer would have been the speed selection, they had been substituted. The autopilot software would expect an answer in knots or kilometres per hour, a much smaller number than a height. Stewart glanced at Hadi who nodded as he entered 2000, meaning two thousand feet. The screen faded slowly and indicated an error as the program shut down.

"What happened then?" Stewart put on the same puzzled expression as Hadi.

"No idea, I entered the desired height as usual."

Hadi had a worried expression.

"Try it again."

They double checked everything and entered everything very carefully with the same result. This was good and bad news, the carnage in Times Square was not about to happen but the terrorists might blame him. When they had listened to McPherson telling him about the security passwords, they had not heard him say about substituting the answers to the height and speed questions.

Hadi was panicking.

" I have to talk to Rula, we will go and find her."

He ushered Stewart out of the room and locked the door. Rula was in an office talking to several men when Hadi gave a brief knock and opened the door.

"Rula I need to talk to you it is urgent."

"Come in." She moved her chair back and waved her arm in a relaxed manner.

"We can't use the Remote-Control Software."

There was a distinct pause before everybody in the room tensed.

"Explain."

"When we began to enter the required data the program shut down."

Rula looked at Stewart.

"Are you sure about this?"

"Hadi double checked everything."

Stewart was not aware of Rula's background, but she was not just an Arab from the desert.

"Do you think McPherson has arranged this?

"Looks that way."

One of the men coughed.

"Can we ask him?"

Rula turned to him slowly.

"We disposed of him."

"Ah."

Rula was thinking, Stewart began to realise that she was definitely not just another Syrian Arab.

She turned and looked directly at Stewart.

"If I am not mistaken you are the world's authority on this software. You can check every line of code and make it work, is that not so?"

Stewart took his time before replying. "Yes, but that could take months."

Hadi interrupted. "But we had only answered one question, so the problem is only that far into the program."

"You know about programs and you will know that even though it was the first question it might be part of something else which is later."

Rula was determined to show the others in the room that she could deal with the problem.

"You will start now and work on it until it is working correctly. Every two days that you waste will be penalised with the death of one of Fishers family. When we run out of them, we will move on to initiating explosions in Washington. Hadi will help you."

"I can't work with somebody else, if I am to do it, I need peace and quiet. He can be in the room but stays quiet".

He knew where the trap was and how to deal with it but intended to ignore it so that he could delay in the hope that something might come up.

There was a brief discussion in Arabic which seemed to end in agreement. She turned back to him.

"Why are you two still here?"

Back in the computer room Hadi produced a laptop.

"I have plenty to do."

Stewart settled down, he had to make it look difficult and time consuming. He knew where exactly in the program he would find the changes that McPherson had made but he did not intend to change them back. Also he had to enter a second password that Hadi was not aware of, it was the password used by the programmers. The password that they had already entered had given them access to use the program but did not allow changes, only the Boeing programmers could do that. In the back of his mind he was trying to figure out how McPherson had obtained that password. Obviously, his snooping around at the Boeing office had been successful. After an hour when he had been giving the impression of checking the program, he decided to test out the second password. He entered it in and spelt it in reverse as they had done with the others. The program immediately shut down, McPherson had not changed that one, he had not expected him to have done so, but it suited him to stop. He gave a loud explanation and Hadi stood up and moved behind his chair.

"What happened?"

"McPherson has made other changes; this is going to take a long time."

"Take a break, we'll get a coffee."

"Good idea."

Hadi locked the door and they headed for the refreshment area. On the way he never stopped talking and asking questions about what he had found.

"You get a coffee while I stretch my legs and get some fresh air."

Hadi nodded his agreement after checking around, there was nowhere for Stewart to go.

"I'll be at the food place please find me there, don't wander off." Hadi had made a joke and knew it.

The surrounding countryside was mainly covered in scrub and small trees with no other signs of habitation. Stewart wandered for a while before sitting down and leaning against a tree. He tried to analyse his situation but kept coming back to the same conclusion. Escape was out of the question, he could string them along, perhaps for a week, he did not doubt for a moment that they would kill Fisher's family if they had to. The view was not particularly good, and he found himself staring at a bush mainly because there was a face in it that was staring at him. The next bush also had a face, that one had a weapon beside it that was pointing at him. He started to sit up, but the first face said something in Arabic that he did not understand.

"Don't shoot." Was all he could think of.

The face answered quietly in accented English.

"Roll onto your stomach and put your hands onto your head."

A fully camouflaged soldier emerged from the bush and crawled over to him and expertly checked him for weapons before rolling him over and checking his front. He was so well camouflaged that Stewart had not seen them as he sat down. They had been there as he approached, and it was only when he focused his vision that he had seen them.

"Are you English?"

"American."

"Are you Stewart Phillips?"

He was astonished, he was lying in the sand in Northern Iraq and somebody knew who he was.

"That's me."

The soldier said something in another language that he did not understand and the second one in the bush replied.

"Start crawling towards me and keep your head down."

"Who are you?"

"Stop talking, we will explain."

As he reached the soldier, he crawled away in front of him, glancing back he could see the other soldier following and removing their marks from the sand. After fifteen or twenty minutes they approached a rock formation and were met by two other soldiers who led them between some large boulders into a shaded place. There were more soldiers there and signs they had been there for some time. Two of the soldiers stayed outside on watch having removed all signs of their movements from the sand.

The soldier who had spoken to him first handed him some water,

"Are you hungry, we have some food?"

"Who are you?"

"Russian army, Speznaz."

"What does that mean?" None of them had any badges on their uniforms, not even badges of rank.

"We are special commandos, similar to your navy Seals or the British SAS." One of the others chipped in.

"They are not as good as us." That produced some laughter and showed the friendly and relaxed atmosphere. One soldier that had not spoken came over and sat next to him, he introduced himself as overseeing the unit.
"We will stay here until they stop looking for you and then we will move back to our base in Syria."

Chapter thirty-four.

Syria.

Several times during the following two hours they had to hunker down as the searchers got close. When this happened the two soldiers who had been on watch outside joined them and they sat in silence. Eventually word was passed back that the search had been halted. They all emerged and formed into groups, Stewart had two soldiers as company and occasionally he caught sight of other groups on both flanks who were guarding his group. They moved on foot westwards, at first, they tried to keep down but after they had covered a fair distance they relaxed. He realised that they were intent on covering the distance to their base camp as quickly as possible. He started feeling the pressure, they were fit and well trained, he was an office worker and started to worry if he could last the distance. He took a drink of water as one of the soldiers came alongside him.
"The River Tigris." He was pointing ahead but he could not see anything at first, then as they got nearer a wide meandering river came into sight. He could not see any boats or a bridge and began to wonder how they would cross. One of the soldiers was using a small handheld radio and he heard the faint noise of a helicopter which grew to a deafening sound as it arrived overhead. He followed the others up a small ramp and the helicopter took off, it was on the ground for no more than two minutes. They landed at a regular airfield which had a variety of aircraft parked out that Stewart did not recognise, they all seemed to be marked with Russian insignia.
"Welcome to Syria." A smart young officer in dress uniform saluted him and took him by car to a large building. Inside he was greeted by two other officers, time to ask questions.
"Can you tell me who you are and where I am and why?"
"You are on a forward military airfield in Syria, we are mainly logistics regiments, but we have some Spetznaz units here, you have met one. We have fighter and bomber units at airfields in other parts of the country as part of our support of President Assad's efforts to defend his country from rebel forces. Your country supports those rebels."
"So why am I here?" They both smiled. "You are a very valuable person Mr Phillips; we need your expertise."
It was not lost on Stewart that he had been working for the United States military until he was captured by Syrian terrorists and now, he was with Russian military.
One of the officers explained.
"We tried to pick you up in the United States, but those Syrians beat us to it, not us personally, we have units working over there. Then you disappeared and we were not sure where you were. Then one of our sources in Tehran reported an American entering the country on a local passport so we thought it might be you. But we lost you again until you were reported crossing into Iraq, from there we could guess where you were going. I immediately dispatched a unit to find you. Their instructions were to do it quietly but if all else failed they were told to destroy that building where they were keeping you."
"Then I walked out for some fresh air and your men acted promptly." He grinned.
"We could not believe it; there you were without a shot being fired. Now we understand that they have worked out what has happened to you and we expect them to attempt a rescue. You were the best thing that had happened for them, they should have taken better care of you."
"Are they close to here?"

"Close, they are all around us, they are the reason we are here. We have sorties from here every day to hunt them down, it is our sport."

"Will they get me?"

"Not a chance, we will be flying you to Moscow by way of Turkey. You leave in the morning."

True to his word next day Stewart boarded a helicopter which took him to a regular airport to board a Russian military transport aircraft. He was accompanied by two Spetznaz officers and some armed soldiers. Before he left the security of the airfield buildings, they provided him with an officer's greatcoat and cap so that he would 'blend in' with the others. He admitted to himself that the coat, cap, and armed guard made him feel safe. The aircraft had delivered supplies to Russian units in Syria and was on its way back to Russia, it was virtually empty and only had the aircrew on board.

One of the Spetznaz officers joked about his rapid promotion, he pointed to the braid on his shoulders.

"You are a general, we are your subordinates and your armed guard."

He did not realise the importance of this until they landed at a civilian airfield in Russia to take on fuel and people in the offices literally got out of his way. While the aircraft was being refuelled everybody on the aircraft moved to a restaurant where there was a choice of food. They had been in the air for more than five hours and during that time they had been supplied with water and tasteless meat with bread. As they relaxed, Stewart slipped the great coat off and sat at a table, he was told to put the great coat back on because other people in the restaurant were looking at him. The captain received a message telling him that the aircraft was ready. He decided to visit the men's room before boarding and when leaving used a different door from the one thew which that he had entered. The doorway was blocked by a stocky bearded man wearing a baseball cap who was speaking rapidly to him.

"I'm sorry I don't understand Russian."

The man switched immediately to English.

"I want to buy your coat and hat. You are obviously not a Russian general and I don't want to know what you are, but I will pay you good money for the coat."

Stewart could not believe how quickly a plan formed in his head. He drew the man back into the toilet area and they stepped into a cubicle. A pile of notes had appeared in the man's hand and he offered them as payment, every time Stewart put on a doubtful expression the amount grew until he knew that he had pushed him far enough. He had no idea how much money was there and whether it was enough to help him escape. He slipped the great coat off and took the cap off the man's head and replaced it with the general's hat. The man gave him the money and Stewart pointed to his black coat, clearly the man had not realised that his coat was part of the deal but after a moment's hesitation slipped it off. He then grabbed the army great coat and put it over his arm and stepped out of the cubicle. The black coat was a good fit and with the cap on his head Stewart cautiously left the men's room, there was no sign of the man, so he quickly left the restaurant and walked away. A bus pulled in and passengers got off and others started to get on, so he joined them. The driver was collecting the fares, so he gave him a note which the driver frowned at, it took him a moment to realise that it was because it was a high denomination. The driver was asking him something so he waved ahead down the road trying to indicate that he wanted to go as far as he could, the driver shrugged and gave him a ticket and a fistful of small notes.

Thirty minutes later the bus arrived at a retail shopping area and drove into a terminus, during the journey he had tried to assess his situation. They would be looking for him and assume that the Syrians had rescued him. The bus had been a stroke of luck because the driver and passengers would not be aware of the search that would be taking place near the restaurant. He walked around for a while seeking inspiration, he had no idea what to do next. He knew he was in Russia but not where he was exactly. As he stood on a pavement, he saw that across the street was a shop that appeared to be selling books, he could see shelves full of them through the glass windows.

"Maybe, they have some books in English or a tourist guide that will help."

He was talking to himself.

It was a library and he started searching for anything that would help. It was the same routine, somebody speaks to you and you answer in English, only in this case the person who spoke to him did not speak English but raised her finger and went away and returned with a schoolgirl.

"I speak English can I help you?"

"Yes, I am lost, do not speak Russian and do not know where I am."

"You are Belaya Dacha which is an outlet mall on the edge of Moscow, how did you arrive here?"

"I flew in with some colleagues." She was looking at his clothes perhaps doubting he flew in.

"We are going to a meeting at the Australian Embassy."

"Ah, you are an Australian."

"I got separated from them at the airport and found a bus which I thought was going to Moscow, but it came here." He had decided not to mention the American Embassy.

"Easily done the airport is such a large place."

"Can I get to the Australian Embassy from here?"

"Very easily, there is a train service, do you have some of our money?"

Stewart produced the notes from his pocket.

"You have a lot of money; you should keep that out of sight, or you may get robbed."

"Where did you learn your English, it is excellent?"

"At school, we had a choice of English, German, French and Chinese. I chose English because one day I hope to visit America but that is impossible at present. I welcome any opportunity to practice my English, thank you." She took him to a display of leaflets and selected two maps.

"You will need to pay for these before you leave."

One of the maps was for the local area and she showed him where he was and how to get to the train station. The other was for the Moscow area and she marked the rail station where he would arrive and underlined the address for the Australian Embassy, he was tempted to ask about the American Embassy but thought better of it.

"You can get a cab from the train, but you would be better walking, with your lack of Russian the driver might take advantage of you."

She wrote some instructions on the map.

"Show this at the station and they will give you the correct ticket."

Stewart thanked her and set off to find the railway station and, on the way, passed many shops including a well-stocked outdoor and camping shop. He had been lucky to get help from the young girl, but he was not naive in thinking it would always be that easy. The search for him might have found a local with a general's topcoat, in which case they would have a good description of what he was now wearing. Also he reasoned because he now knew that he was close to Moscow they might suspect he would make for the United States Embassy. He decided he would check out the embassy looking for a reception committee outside. If there was, he would have to think of a different way of getting out of Russia.

Stewart emerged from the outdoor shop having bought a pair of walking boots, new trousers with pockets down the leg, an anorak type coat, a woollen cap, a sports shirt without any writing on the front and a haversack. He found the station easily but before buying a ticket he visited the men's room and changed clothes. With the woollen hat in place and the hood from the coat pulled over it he was confident that he would stand casual scrutiny. His only remaining problem was language and he could not do anything about that. He dumped all the wrapping material and the black jacket and cap in a trash can, the words the girl had written on his map had worked and he was soon on board a train that stopped at the terminus in Moscow. He left the train with a group of other travellers, keeping his head down he walked slowly and avoided looking around which would be a sign of nervousness. As he crossed the concourse, he saw small groups of armed soldiers and a few men who were doing their best to appear inconspicuous, he realised they might always be there and not necessarily looking for him. He walked confidently out of the station without looking at his map until he saw a couple of well-dressed businessmen who he approached.

"Excuse me can you point me towards the US Embassy?" He was taking a chance, but he had little choice. They both reacted as though they directed English speakers every day and looked at his map before giving him clear directions. His only other option had been to wander about looking for a stars and stripes flag. He entered the street where the US Embassy was located, he was surprised how big it was. The entrances were on the other side of the road, so he crossed over and with his hands in his coat pockets he strolled slowly along. As he got nearer, he could see a car parked in the roadway, he thought he could see two men inside and there was a third leaning on the car and talking to those inside. He managed to resist the urge to turn and run, they would have caught him before he reached the end of the road. He tried to tell himself that they were there for another reason, but their manner suggested otherwise.

There were two entrances, one for vehicles and one for pedestrians, both ended up at the front of the building. He passed the vehicle entrance and the parked car and without increasing his speed turned up the footpath. He was nearly at the building when he heard the car engine start and the car turned into the vehicular entrance. It was racing to cut him off before he reached the building, he had to get there before them, he just made it as he sprinted up the steps.

At the top there was a security station which was manned by two United States soldiers, they had an iron gate that was closed.

"I'm a US citizen and need help." He could hear footsteps behind him, he indicated behind him.

"These men are Russian secret service and they are trying to detain me."

"Can we see your passport sir?"

"It's at home in Washington."

The two men who were out of breath tried to take hold of him but one of the guards produced a submachine gun from behind the railings. The Russians immediately released him, and one produced an identity card.

"We are here to arrest this man, he is an enemy of our country, please stand aside."

"You cannot arrest him here; he is on American soil."

The Russian was not giving up.

"We are dealing with an urgent security matter and need to detain this man."

"You do not have any authority here, please return to the roadway immediately."

Some other soldiers had appeared behind them and one led Stewart through the gate and used a hand scanner to check for weapons. One of the Russians was using a radio for further instructions.

"This way sir." They took him to an elevator which carried him to the fourth floor where three men were waiting for him.

"Who are you?" The older of the three was asking the questions.

"Stewart Phillips, I work for ... "He was interrupted.

"We thought you might be, we have had a CIA notice to look out for you."

Stewart was taken into an office where he explained himself and what had happened to him after he was abducted in Baltimore. They were joined by a young man who explained that both the front and rear entrances to the Embassy had been blocked by soldiers. No vehicles were being allowed in and those leaving were being searched, a garbage truck had been searched as it left.

"They are taking you very seriously, we've never had this level of interference before."

There was a lengthy telephone conversation.

"That was the Ambassador, he has contacted Washington and is awaiting instructions. In the meantime you are a prisoner here and we are to make you comfortable."

The irony was not lost on Stewart, he had been made comfortable in Baltimore and in Iraq, this one would surely be the most comfortable. He was taken up to a higher floor which was more like a hotel.

"You are not actually restricted in your movements, but we urge you not to wander about too much, we might need to talk to you. You will find some areas have restricted access and a card is needed."

"Understood."

His 'room' was a small apartment with a living room, bedroom, bathroom and kitchen, there were instructions on the inside of the door which told him where the restaurant was and the best way to escape if the was a fire. A leather-bound book on a coffee table told him how to use the telephone and the television, he decided he was in a Holiday Inn. He tried to figure out the local time and decided that an evening meal was called for and was about to leave the room when one of the three men that he had met earlier knocked on his door.

"Ambassador's compliments Mr Phillips will you join him for dinner?"

"Fine, when will that be?"

"Now sir."

The Ambassador did not live in a Holiday Inn type apartment, he introduced himself as Craig Fellowes and explained that his wife was away visiting friends and his children were dining separately. There were four of them for dinner and an excellent meal was served by the embassy staff. It was obvious that the Ambassador wanted to be brought up to date.

"I had heard about this anti hijack equipment but not this remote-control system, is it a variation?"

"I'm not sure which came first Ambassador, but they are both in use."

"Has the anti-hijack system actually been used to save lives?"

"Not as far as I know even though there have been opportunities."

Stewart got the impression that the Ambassador and the others were curious but anxious to not get too involved. They were interrupted by the CIA man that Stewart had met earlier who brought a message that the Ambassador read and then passed to the others.

"This message is from Washington they are pleased that you are safe, they say the Russians will go to great lengths to detain you."

The CIA man added that a means of escape has just presented itself and that he should grab his things and meet him at the ground floor by the elevator. Stewart's things consisted of his coat and his haversack. He was led to the rear of the building where an ambulance was waiting with its doors open and a medic was holding some fluorescent medical clothing for him. The CIA man explained.

"One of the staff has just suffered a heart attack, he is being brought down now. This is a private ambulance that is going to a private hospital."

"Won't they search the ambulance?"

"Hopefully not, we have organised this so quickly that they will not expect anything. If they do search the ambulance get out as quickly as possible and run back, he will help you." He was pointing to a young man who was also dressed in fluorescent medical clothing. A stretcher was brought from the elevator with an unconscious man on it and was loaded into the ambulance. Stewart and the other agent climbed into the vehicle and the doors closed and the ambulance moved. Their exit through the rear gates onto the road was blocked by a small truck and a soldier came to each front window and studied the inside of the ambulance before calling out an instruction. The truck blocking the exit moved and they drove slowly out through the gates.

"I wondered if they might notice that there are two more medical attendants in the rear."

The driver explained.

"Different soldiers, we came in through the front gates".

Stewart knew that he should feel safe but there was a nagging thought that this would be an excellent way for the Russians to get him out of the Embassy. All he could do was wait. It was a short drive before the ambulance turned down a private road that led to a modern building. The paramedics were out quickly and dealt with the stretcher. The CIA man stripped off his fluorescent jacket and indicated that he should do the same and that they should stay in the ambulance. A porter came out of the hospital and closed the rear doors of the ambulance which drove quietly around the building. At the rear there was a parked car and the ambulance parked next to it. After a slight pause the side door of the ambulance opened and they transferred to the car, leaving just the driver in the ambulance which moved away. There was another pause and the car drove away from the hospital. They followed a country road until they reached a lay by where a second car waited for them. Apart from the driver there was one other man who was seated in the rear. Stewart slid in next to him and turned to him, it was a surprise, it was Spencer Coltrane.

"Coltrane, what are you doing here?"

"Holding your hand."

"When and how did you get here?"

"I've been here a few days waiting for you to arrive."

Stewart could think of a load of questions but decided they could wait.

"It was decided that you needed some help and it would be better if came from somebody you know and trust. You do trust me don't you." He was grinning.

"I'm relieved to see you."

"I'll explain everything when we are on the train."

"Train, where are we going?" Coltrane held a finger to his lips.

The car headed towards the city centre and stopped at the main railway station. They were met by another man who held up three rail tickets. Coltrane led the way into the station restaurant and ordered three coffees. The agent with the tickets advised them that they had twenty minutes to wait before their train arrived.

"Where are we going?"

"St Petersburg."

"How long will that take?"

"About five hours."

"Why St Petersburg?"

"It's difficult to get into Russia without being noticed but it's just as hard to get out. Land borders are particularly difficult, seaports are the best way, Russia has two, Vladivostok on the Pacific coast and St Petersburg which gives access to the Baltic. Vladivostok is too far away so we have arranged to join a freighter that is leaving St Petersburg."

"It will be even harder without a passport, mine is in my apartment in Washington."

"I have two passports for you, one in your own name the other is fictitious. We won't be showing them to anybody, we will leave quietly but we have them if we need them."

Stewart was feeling exposed sitting in the restaurant with people milling around them. "We would have been safer waiting in the car. We will be spotted."

"I hope so."

Chapter Thirty-five.

When the train arrived, they boarded and were pointed to their seats by the attendant, the train left on time. Coltrane leaned against him and explained.

"We get off at the next stop, at the very last minute as the guard is blowing his whistle. When the train reaches St Petersburg it will be met by an officer from the ship, in the crowd there will be three sailors who will join him in a taxi which will take them to the dock. In the meantime we will be in a car going somewhere else. Hopefully, Russian security will be concentrating on this train and the ship."

Stewart now understood why they had sat in public at the station.

It all went to plan at the next station, passengers left the train and others boarded. At the last minute as the doors were being slammed, they stood up and went to the nearest door. Coltrane kept them there until the guard blew his whistle and they opened the door and stepped onto the platform. They stood still as the guard slammed the door and the train went past them.

"Where is the other guy who had the tickets?"

"He stayed on and will be questioned at the other end, creating further confusion."

They exited the station and found a car waiting for them, which drove to another railway station, it was a long drive.

"Where do these trains go to?"

"Belarus."

"I can't believe how much effort has been put in to save my skin."

"There's more at stake than your skin."

They had a cabin with two bunks and a bathroom, Coltrane had everything organised.

"This is a seventeen-hour journey, no need to leave this cabin, our meals will be delivered here. There was a light tap on the door and Coltrane let another man into the cabin who handed over rail tickets. Coltrane reached inside his coat and produced a United States passport. Stewart inspected the passport and the ticket; they were both in the name of Michael Hardy.

"Mike, you are a travel writer for tourist magazines at home, you won't be questioned in any detail. Just be relaxed if anybody speaks to you."

"Relaxed, I don't think I will ever be relaxed again. Do they speak English?"

Coltrane grinned. "Is this the first time you have been out of the States?"

Stewart nodded.

"Could be the last."

"English is spoken everywhere by a lot of people."

"Yeh! Including Syria and Iraq."

"I don't know about them I haven't been there yet."

Stewart was not sure that Coltrane knew that he had arrived in Russia through those countries.

The compartment was clean and comfortable but slightly old fashioned, the settled down for the long ride. Stewart was curious about how and why Coltrane has joined him.

" Time for you to explain your appearance here, I'm grateful of course but don't understand."

"We lost you in Baltimore, we think they took you from their building to the house next door but there was no sign of how they did that. Not that it mattered as you had completely disappeared."

"They took me to an airport, and I was put on a flight to Tehran."

"We know that now. One of our resident agents reported that an American had landed on a flight from Washington, He was the only non-Arab on the flight. Unfortunately, he could not get a photograph, but we thought it might be you."

Stewart recalled how careful the Syrians had been as they did not want Iranian interference.

"We lost you again until we had positive advice you had crossed into Iraq and I was dispatched to get to the Qasad base before you. I got there the day after you and we lost you again. "

"The Russians had got me, a Spetznaz unit based in Syria."

"Nasty people."

"They were alright with me."

"Then we lost you again before you turned up at our Embassy in Moscow."

"Still you will get full marks for effort."

Coltrane was beaming, but Stewart was curious about something Coltrane had said earlier

"When we got onto this train you said it was a seventeen-hour journey, where is it going?"

"Minsk in Belarus."

"So, I can barely figure out the map in my head, but I think that means we will be heading west and the train to St Petersburg would have been going north west."

"That's about right, stop worrying we have everything arranged."

"Tell me the full story."

Coltrane screwed up his face while he decided.

"OK, we get off the train in Minsk and then travel by car into Poland, we can cross the border using our fake US passports. Poland is a European Community country which gives us access to all the European Community countries, there are no internal borders. We will travel by train into Germany, to Ramstein which is a US Army base that supplies all the US military in Europe. From there we can catch a returning US Airforce freighter back to the states, job done. Even allowing for delays we will be home within a few days."

"Sounds good to me."

Stewart realised that he was being optimistic, and a lot of things could change. He suspected that Coltrane was thinking alone the same lines but did not say so. He decided a sleep would be a good idea and stretched out on one of the bunks. The trains whistle woke him up, he had no idea how long he had been asleep. The train was stopping, and Coltrane was looking out of the window.

"What's happening?"

"No idea I'll find out."

He stepped out into the corridor and Stewart could hear him talking in Russian to somebody, it was a short conversation and Coltrane returned to the compartment and locked the door.

"Truck broken down on a level crossing, somebody is working on it."

The train came to a complete halt and they could see people on the ground outside.

"We'll stay inside, I don't like this."

He opened his travel bag and brought out a pistol which he checked.

"I don't suppose that you have a weapon?"

Stewart shook his head.

"Do you think we should move to another compartment, if this is an attempt to detain us, they will know which apartment we are in."

"Good idea, but there may not be any empty ones."

"Doesn't matter, if there are occupants, we will join them. At least we will have warning if they come to this compartment."

Coltrane went back into the corridor and returned quickly.

"There is an empty one further down. "

He grabbed his bag and led the way; the corridor was empty, and the compartment did not have any signs that it was in use. They stepped inside and slid the door shut but did not lock it. They stood near the door, listening and heard the truck start up, then the train whistle sounded possibly to tell the passengers that had alighted when the train stopped that they should board. The sound of shuffling feet came from the corridor and it was obvious that somebody was waiting there. Coltrane gently eased the door open.

"Three men and a guard outside our compartment. The men are armed and talking in a language that I do not understand, wait a minute I don't think they are Russian but one of them speaks to the guard in Russian."

He silently slid the door to close it.

"They know we are not in the compartment and I think they are waiting for us to return, we are trapped. That truck was a setup, someone has boarded the train and is looking for us. We would have been better off if we had got off the train and walked away."

Stewart thought the longer this goes on it will become more difficult for them.

"I think we should confront them now when they are not expecting it."

The train whistle sounded two shot blasts; the driver was getting impatient.

Coltrane nodded his agreement and slid the door open by a small amount. Coltrane peered through the small gap.

"Two of them and the guard have their backs to us, only the one facing us has his weapon trained this way. I going to take him out first then deal with the other two who will have to turn around to use their weapons."

He slid the door open as quietly as he could and stepped out. The nearest one who had his back to them heard the door and turned around exposing the second one who was facing them who Coltrane shot in the head. Coltrane fired a burst that hit the guard and the other one that had his back to them. He had taken out two of them very quickly, unfortunately the guard had been hit. The remaining one dropped his weapon and put his hands up, he was grinning. It was then that they heard a polite cough behind them. Stewart turned first and could not believe what he saw.

"Stewart how nice to see you again."

Rula Asad was standing in a crouched position with a sub machine gun pointing at them.

"You left me in Syria without saying goodbye, that was not nice when you consider all I had done for you."

She was looking past them at the pile of bodies and the survivor who was picking up his weapon. Coltrane was trying to come to terms with the reversal of their fortune.

"Do you know this woman?"

"I met her in Syria, she is with Qasad, the terrorist group. They took me hostage in Baltimore and moved me to Iran and then to Syria before the Russians intervened."

"And now we have you back."

She was studying Coltrane.

"Who is this?"

"He is a local agent from the United States, he is of no consequence."

"He just killed two of our men." As she spoke, she raised the sub machine gun and Stewart stepped in front of her.

"Don't shoot him."

"Why not?"

"Because I like him, and he is a good person and he shot them to protect me."

She thought for minute and spoke to the remaining gunman, in Russian, who pushed Coltrane into the compartment, collected the various weapons and closed the door.

Chapter thirty-six.

The three of them left the train and walked to the front of the locomotive and as they did so the truck moved off the line and stopped a short distance away. Rula signalled to the locomotive driver to go, the train started moving and it disappeared down the line and it was soon out of sight around a curve. Stewart looked around, they were on an empty hillside, no people, and no houses. He was pushed into the truck cab and Rula joined him, the gunman climbed onto the back. The driver looked young and smiled a lot, by contrast the truck was old, it was a wreck. He hoped they were not going far as it was uncomfortable and noisy. They approached a stand of small trees and parked next to it was a Mercedes people carrier which they transferred to and left the truck behind the trees.

"Where are we going to?"

She wagged a finger at him.

"I've learnt that the less that you know the better it is for me."

"Are we going to the Qasad headquarters in Syria?" She was silent with a sullen stare.

"You know of course that that building and everybody there were totally destroyed by bombers, the day after you left."

"I did not know that, surely you don't think I was responsible."

"Weren't you?"

"A day later I was already on a plane to Moscow, and the Spetznaz guys already knew what that building was, they went there to take me hostage." She did not answer.

"If everybody in the Qasad building was killed why are you still here?"

"I was out looking for you, we did not know that the Russians were that close. I thought that you could be hiding in the countryside and that you would come out of hiding if you saw me. I watched the bombers destroy the building and that told me that you were with the Russians."

"How did you find out where I was?"

"I guessed that if the Russians had you, they would take you very quickly to Moscow, we have some people here who were able to confirm this."

"But we switched trains you could not have anticipated that."

"That is true so we put people on the train, we had time to organise this because you spent a while in the station cafeteria. Those people are still on that train and they reported the fact that you got off at the next station. I was in Moscow when I was alerted, and I made a lucky guess as to where you may be headed and caught the train in Moscow, I watched you board and called to somebody ahead to organise the truck and stop the train. It worked well."

She smiled at him. "We are together again."

The driver was driving confidently without using a map, he knew the area very well. He was in the back with Rula and must have fallen asleep and he woke with a start as the car hit a bump.

"You were sleeping, does nothing trouble you?"

"I was trying to work out how you are going to get me out of Russia, we are a long way from Syria."

She laughed. "We are not going to Syria; at the moment we are heading south towards Turkey, but we will not leave Russia."

"How far will we be travelling?"

"Twenty hours, we will not stop but will change drivers."

She smiled again and, in a flash, he realised what Qasad was planning.

"You intend to operate the system from inside Russia."

"We have acquired two suitable locations and will set up two control centres there."

"Two."

"Safety in numbers, if Moscow manages to locate one, only one will be active at any one time, the other will teach them a lesson, the Kremlin and other important buildings will simply disappear."

Stewart remembered that back home in the States there were two control centres, it made sense.

She was laughing and touched hm on his face.

"We need you to train some operators."

"Are you forgetting that we can't actually use the software?"

"I have every faith in you being able to solve that problem."

They drove most of the day with the occasional stop for fuel and take way food and it was turning dusk when he saw water ahead, Rula explained.

"Black Sea, those bright lights on our left are Sochi, we are nearly there."

He had heard of Sochi it was a holiday resort, he recalled that the Olympics had been held there. They turned onto a minor road and shortly afterwards into a farmyard. During the journey he had been assessing his situation. Qasad must be well supported and be well funded. They had been clever, by basing their operation in Russia they were in a secure situation, until Qasad used the system most countries would think that the United States was still in control. When it was used, they would be frightened to confront whoever was using it because of the fear of retaliation, there would be no reason to suspect that the operation was based in Russia. That reasoning would also apply to the Russians themselves. With those thoughts he realised that any chances of Qasad's plans being thwarted could be down to him alone.

Stewart needed to escape again but realised that he could only do so when he was certain that Qasad could not use the system. He also knew that if he made changes to the software, they might be able to deal with that by finding somebody who could find the changes and reverse them. His best chance was to delete large blocks from the software and replace it with fake code, that way anybody who tried to take over would have to find the fake code to replace and then try to change it with correct code. The only way to do that would be to have access to the master copy at Boeing which would be difficult. Also he realised that Rula had a second copy, he had to alter that in the same way.

His own safety had to be taken into consideration, Qasad would go to any lengths to keep him safe but when he had trained some of their operators, he was expendable. He would have to be careful and one problem that he was not in control of concerned him, he could be rescued before he had made the changes. Rula did not know that Coltrane was a Russian speaker, she had put him in an unlocked compartment while they left the train. Coltrane would have been on the next train back into Moscow and heading for the US Embassy, he would have been working on locating him while they were driving down to Sochi.

They arrived at a farmhouse which was an excellent base for Qasad's operation, apart from the house itself there was a large barn that had been converted into accommodation. That was for the Syrians who looked after the property and the needs of the occupants including cooking and laundry. They all spoke Russian and dressed as farm workers and never carried weapons but there must have been some weapons hidden in easily accessible places. Upon arrival Stewart was supplied with rough clothes so that he looked like the others. Any unexpected visitors would have no reason to believe that it was not a working farm. It was not a working farm; he suspected the land had been sold for development. They even had some items of farm equipment, such as tractors, that were moved around so that they gave the impression that they were being used. Satellite surveillance would not identify the real use of the farm. He had expected there to be a unit of guards, possibly based in the barn but there were none. He thought about this until he realised that the location was expendable, if it were discovered it would be destroyed by aircraft from Sochi Airport in minutes. That way a working system would not fall into the hands of any opposition, it was the reason for the second control centre which was probably located hundreds of miles away. These thoughts prompted the realisation that it was the same set up in the United States, the controls were in dedicated villages that could disappear if threatened.

Immediately Stewart was set to work where he left off in Syria, he had to check the whole program, a mammoth task. As before he was given an assistant, essentially to keep an eye on him, Mo was older than Hadi who he had worked with in Iraq. Hadi had probably died when the Russians had destroyed the headquarter building. Mo seemed to understand programming which was not important because Stewart would not be allow him to become too familiar with the software. They worked in a room on the end of the building, which was locked, and Mo had the key along with the key to the cupboard that housed the computer.

Rula had been specific when she instructed him.

"You will work here, Mo is in charge and you will keep him up to date with any progress and he will report to me, do not get any thoughts about walking away as you did in Iraq where there were Russians to help you. Here you are surrounded by Russians, but they cannot help you. They are local, ordinary people who are as far removed from Moscow as they can get, many resent Moscow's powers, which is why we are based here. Also we will be keeping a closer watch on you this time."

"I know when I am well off, good weather, good food and accommodation, if you leave me alone, I will do what you ask."

She was smiling he had just told her what she wanted to hear.

"I'm glad to hear it."

"You can concentrate on killing some American soldiers."

"Why would we want to do that? The Americans and the American military are our friends and allies, we love them."

"So why do you want this means of remotely controlling aircraft?"

"It is too good an opportunity to miss. Once we have it working, we will talk again with your government and our agreement will change."

"Can we have dinner tonight?"

She laughed out loud at his rapid change of subject.

"Why not, there will be ten others with us."

"That won't matter, it will be nice to have a relaxed conversation with you."

As she walked away, he thought that the discussion went well. He had not realised how few terrorists were based there and he had made friends with her which could affect her judgement. To test that he called after her.

"Can I go swimming? I swam a lot in the Pacific back home."

"I don't see why not, I will have to arrange for somebody to be with you, I might join you,"

He planned to start as soon as possible and go as often as he could. He wanted to know the best way down to the beach and if there were any boats that he could borrow. Escaping overland would be difficult but by sailing north he suspected there were more opportunities, but first he had to deal with the changes to the software.

Chapter thirty-seven.

Coltrane landed awkwardly when he was pushed into the compartment, he was on his feet quickly and tried the door very gently. He was surprised to find it was not locked but he did not open it as he was not sure what the situation was in the corridor. He pressed his ear to the door and listened, above the noise of the train he could not detect any noises in the corridor, he opened the door very carefully at first and then sufficient to get his head out, there were three bodies in the corridor and there was blood everywhere. Apart from the bodies there was nobody in the corridor, so he stepped out and slid the door closed. He had to get away from the scene of carnage before he became involved, first he checked the victims to ensure they were dead and then he collected his case from the compartment that they originally used. He transferred to the next carriage and started looking for an empty compartment. He had just found one when the train slowed and stopped, it was a large station and he got off quickly amongst other passengers and showed his ticket at the end of the platform. He headed for the ticket office and bought a ticket for Moscow and was advised that one was leaving in ten minutes from the next platform.

It arrived on time and he boarded and sat watching the activity on the adjacent platform. Very quickly it became crowded with police and medics and the access to the platform was sealed, he had done the right thing by getting off the platform straight away. After he left the train in Moscow, he found a taxi rank and went to the American Embassy where he explained the situation to the Ambassador, who did not realise that Stewart had been taken hostage, he assumed that he was safe somewhere.

"Who has Phillips and where are they taking him?"

"I think they were Syrians, but they could be working for somebody else, and I have no idea where they have taken him."

That was his next task, to trace where Stewart had gone or more correctly guess where he had been taken. He sat down with a large coffee and tried to reason it out. Stewart had identified the young woman as a member of a Syrian terrorist organisation Qasad that he had met in Iraq. The train that they were on was going to Minsk, which was not in the direction of Syria, if they wanted to go to Minsk, they would not have abducted Stewart at the start of the journey. They would have waited to the end of the journey to make it easier for them. Then he had a thought.

"We were still in Russia when they stopped the train, that's where they will be. I bet they tell the Russians that they are ordinary Syrian citizens, no mention of Qasad. The Russians are allies of the Syrian monarchy and will help them. "He was talking to himself. "They are travelling south towards Turkey and then back to Syria, but they are still in Russia."

He could not narrow it down any closer to that. He put in a diplomatic call from the US Embassy in Moscow to the US Embassy in Ankara, Turkey asking them to notify him if either Stewart Phillips or Michael Hardy arrived in Turkey. Stewart did not have a passport, the two that he had organised were still in his pocket. If Stewart was forced to identify himself, he might use the Michael Hardy name to avoid explaining who Stewart Phillips is to hostile inquirers. Knowing it was a waiting game, he felt he had no other way of locating Stewart so he drew up a list of adjacent countries that he might be taken to, there were six. He decided to contact the United States Embassy in each of those countries and ask them to notify him if Phillips or Hardy arrived there.

"I'm clutching at straws here." He muttered knowing that would only work if Stewart were transported by road or rail, if his capturers decided to fly him somewhere his landing place could be anywhere. He also had to allow for him not being seen by the immigration service of the country that he landed in. He stood up quickly.

"What if they decide not to take him out of Russia? They could hunker down anywhere in the country while we wear ourselves out searching everywhere, everywhere being any country in the world."

There was a light tap on the office door.

"Are you alright in there?"

He must have shouted,

"Yes, sorry I got a bit excited."

He realised he had stumbled on a probable answer, if they stayed in Russia but out of sight, they would be safe. They would go south so that when the hunt had died down, they would only have to cross Turkey to reach Syria. He sat down slowly as he realised it was a good answer, but it did not make the task of finding Stewart any easier, Russia was a big country.

Chapter Thirty-eight.

Somewhere on the Black Sea coast.

Stewart knew he had to get started but he took his time, there was nothing to be gained by rushing and the farm was a pleasant place to work, it was quiet with no traffic noise. He was left on his own except for Mo who showed interest in the software but not sufficient to understand it, he became certain that Mo was mainly a guard with some computer knowledge. He tested this theory from time to time by mentioning some issue or other and waiting for Mo to comment, he never did. Stewart was working slowly but steadily and had already changed a large section of code and also made other changes to the security access so that even if they used the second copy the program would still fail to operate. He could not risk asking Rula if he could update her copy as she may have become suspicious. If he went outside to stretch his legs Mo went with him, except for two occasions when he found another Syrian already in the yard waiting for him. They were being more careful than they had been in Iraq. He knew that he had to build up a picture of the daily life of everybody, most of them did not appear to have a function except as a member of Qasad. It was obvious that he would not be able to slip away during the day and night-time was not an option. His room overlooked the front of the building and the farmyard and during the night he could hear movement, they had guards posted. Clearly there was no ideal time, he would have to take his chances. His first task was to find out where he was, Mo had clearly been instructed to tell him nothing and Rula was reluctant to help even when exchanging small talk.

"How is your room?"

"I like it, it has a pleasant view from my window. I can see right down the lake."

"That's good." She had a slight smile on her face she knew he was trying to get information. He had seen large ships on the horizon and knew that it was a sea. They had not crossed a border and been travelling south so he felt it must be the Mediterranean, but his knowledge of the region was not great. Most of the men that he was in contact with spoke English, so he tried with some of them.

"The Mediterranean seems to be very calm today."

They did not answer which meant that they had been told not to give him any information or they did not know if that were the Mediterranean, he decided to back off for a while, he would find out in due course. I happened quicker than he expected Rula told him what he wanted to know.

"I am advised that you have been asking questions about the sea, it is the Black Sea. Now I do not know what is going through that head of yours but do not get the idea that you can escape. There are no Spetznaz forces here to help you, you are still in Russia and like everybody else they are looking for you in every place except Russia. Please be satisfied with what you have got, you have comfortable accommodation and good food. I can easily put you in a cage, a secure room and life will be different. We have plenty of people to watch you, we know where you are, all the time."

He nodded. "Thank you, I just wanted to know."

Rula had agreed he could go swimming so he decided to do that and see how it worked out, he suspected that Mo would accompany him even if he did not go in the water. It was looking likely that he would have to deal with Mo, hopefully without seriously hurting him. He found Rula and told her he wanted to go swimming.

"Fine, I will see you in the yard in an hours' time, I will bring you an extra pair of trousers and a shirt. You will need a towel from your room."

At the right time he stood up from the computer and advised Mo that he was going swimming. Mo's reaction was to produce a bundle of clothes and a towel.

"So am I."

They went into the yard where Rula was waiting, she was dressed in fatigues and was carrying two spare sets and a towel. She was going swimming with them which was unusual for an Arab woman. After leaving the farm through the main gate they turned left, away from the sea, and after a short walk that took them behind the farm, they turned down a dusty track. This puzzled him as he would have turned right, he reasoned that there was no way through to the water by going in that direction. Very quickly they reached the water's edge and he was surprised to see a small jetty and a boat tied up alongside. He had not been able to see this from the window, Rula produced a bunch of keys from her pocket and unlocked the cabin door and pocketed the keys. They left their towels and spare clothes on the deck.

"We can dry ourselves and change in there when we come out."

She was a good swimmer; Mo paddled a little and walked out until the water reached his waist and walked out after a couple of minutes. He stayed in the water with Rula for another fifteen to twenty minutes. Mo was already standing on the jetty; he had changed from his wet trousers and was dry. It was clear that he had not wanted to go swimming but had been told to do so. Rula changed next and emerged from the cabin with the towel around her head, he changed next. They were waiting for him as he climbed onto the jetty and Rula jumped down and relocked the cabin. On the walk back he chatted to Rula about the weather.

Stewart had learned a lot on that first swimming visit to the sea. The boat was a bonus and on subsequent visits he was accompanied by Mo and another Syrian as Rula did not go again. He went into the sea on his own and the two Syrians sat on the jetty smoking. This was a bonus because they could not see him when he was changing on the boat from where they were sitting. There were two fuel cans tied down on the deck and when he tapped them with his knuckle, he could tell they were full, likewise the fuel tank that was part of the engine gave the same sound. There was sufficient fuel to get somewhere, he was not sure where. He went swimming every day for a week which seemed to irritate Mo, but he never spoke about it, on each occasion he took a plastic bottle of water with him and hid it in the cabin. When Rula had the key in her hand on her first visit he had clearly seen that there was only one key on the ring, as there were locks on the fuel cans, the engine and a chain fastening the boat to the jetty the other keys must be on the boat. On every visit he searched but could not find them in the limited time he had while drying and changing. He would have to carry on swimming until he did.

During one of his searches he found two maps, one had pencil lines on it showing journeys to places on the Turkish coast and one to Istanbul, this answered three important questions, firstly that the boat had sufficient range to reach Turkey. Secondly it told him exactly where he was, the pencil lines converged to a point north of Sochi and lastly that he had to steer due south and he would avoid Georgia and reach the Turkish coast. He still had to find the keys, luck came to the rescue, when leaving the boat he steadied himself with his hand on top of the door frame, he had checked there but only visually. They were there in a recess, he quickly checked that there was the right number and replaced them. All he had to find was where the single key to the farm building was hidden, he had noticed that Mo had entered the front entrance with the key when they returned from swimming and come back out without it. He had no reason to enter the building through the front entrance, but he had to if he was going to find where the key was kept. On every occasion that he was outside he went back into the building through the front entrance, he found that there were two doors in the hallway, one was to the dining room and the other was a cupboard. Mo had not gone into the dining room as he would have seen him through the window, the key was kept in the cupboard. His difficulty was that every time he was outside Mo was with him and followed him back in. For a week he tried to get time in the cupboard without Mo following him without success.

The sound of rain woke him and the noise of loud talking, it was torrential rain, and everybody was in the dining room he went outside and they were all sheltering. Because he had not come down to breakfast it would be assumed, he was still in bed. He re-entered the house through the front entrance, the door to the dining room was closed and he was able to go into the cupboard without being seen. His heart was pounding as he entered the cupboard, if he were caught now it would be obvious what he was doing. The cupboard was a large one and it was fully of household paraphernalia, he cast his eye around not knowing where to start and his gaze saw a nail in the door frame with the keys hanging on it. He snatched them up and looked out of the door, there was nobody in the hall, it was too easy. For a second he had to make his mind up, should he put the keys back and plan his escape or should he take the opportunity that the heavy rain had given him. They were still talking in loud voices in the dining room.

He dashed through the front door and kept close to the building while he circled the house and went down the lane to the jetty. He was soaking wet, but it did not matter. The other keys were still in the recess over the door and with trembling hands he undid the chain that fastened the boat to the jetty. It was also tied up with two ropes and he disconnected them, one key had Suzuki cast into it, and it plugged into the engine. A quick check to find the fuel tap which he turned on and he turned the key hoping everything worked. The engine started immediately and with a quick glance up the jetty to check nobody was watching he sat at the controls in the cabin and opened the throttle. The boat moved immediately, and he set the course, by the compass, to due west and headed out to sea. He had decided not to turn until he was over the horizon that way if anybody pursued him, they would not know which way he had gone. He was looking back to see when the coastline disappeared, and it happened earlier than expected due to the heavy rain.

He turned onto a southerly course and at this point the full impact of what he had done occurred to him. He had never sailed a boat before and while he had a good knowledge of aircraft navigation, boats were something else, there were rocks in the sea. The boat engine droned and the rain died down, he looked around and could not see another boat. As a precaution he put on a life jacket and examined some flares that he had found in a locker, the clouds rolled back, and the sun appeared. It was a nice day for escaping except he had no plan. Studying the map did not help as he had no idea where he would make landfall in Turkey, if it would be a port, he would have difficulty docking, but he felt he would manage. Then there was officialdom to deal with, he had no papers or a passport, he decided that he would use the Michael Hardy name. That should bring some action from the US Embassy. If there was not a port, he would beach the boat and walk away knowing that he would have to contact the US embassy at some point.

He was awakened from his thoughts by a huge roar and the boat pitched to the left, a large grey ship was going past him on his right, it was turning in a large circle and coming back at high speed. It approached again from the rear and slowed to his speed. A sailor was on deck with a megaphone and two other sailors lay either side of him, they were armed. The one with the megaphone was saying something which he did not understand, he cupped his hands around his mouth and shouted back.
"English."
There was some discussion on the deck of the other ship before it moved closer and he was advised to heave to, he switched the engine off and the ship came really close and an inflatable boat with

four armed men on board appeared from the other side of the ship. They came alongside and boarded his boat, because of their weapons he raised his arms. Two of them kept him covered while the other two searched the boat which took all of two minutes. It occurred to him that the boat could have been used for smuggling and even worse drug smuggling, if they found any evidence he would be in real trouble. The searchers returned shaking their heads and the atmosphere improved with one of them with more stripes on his uniform taking charge, he spoke in good English.

"Papers for you and the boat please."

"I don't have any."

Stewart had been studying their uniforms, the ship had few markings and flew a flag that he did not recognise.

"Are you Georgian?"

"We are the Coastguard service of Turkey; you are in Turkish waters and you are under arrest."

Within minutes he was transferred first to the inflatable boat and then to the coastguard boat and two sailors were left aboard his boat to sail it away. He was put into a cabin with two senior looking officers one of them sat at a desk and made notes while the other studied him closely.

Chapter thirty-nine.

The older one was asking the questions; earlier Stewart had decided to use the Michael Hardy alias that Coltrane has created but faced with these two officers who were about to interrogate him he had second thoughts. If they were able to check the authenticity of that name, he could be charged with entering the country illegally by using a false name. On the other hand if he used his own name, Stewart Phillips, it might be recognised, and Turkey might decide not to hand him over. Almost certainly the Turkish military would have heard about the remote hijack software and could decide that they wanted it. The US Embassy would recognise the Michael Hardy name because the false passport had been issued legally and, hopefully, they would rescue him.

The first question decided for him.

"What is your name?".

"Michael Hardy."

"You don't have any documents to show us."

"I'm afraid not."

"Where are they?"

"I don't know."

"Where did you enter our country?"

"I sailed from Russia and I entered your country at the point that you intercepted me."

"Who owns the boat?"

"I don't know."

"Where did you sail from?"

"Somewhere in Russia near Sochi but I don't know exactly."

"Where were you heading?"

"I don't know, somewhere on the Turkish coast. Can you notify the United States Embassy in Ankara that I am here and need their help?"

"Where did you enter Russia?"

"I flew into Moscow." He was confident with that answer as it would be hard to verify with the Russians.

"What was the purpose of your visit?"

"I write tourist books and I flew into Iran to take photos and I was kidnapped and taken to Iraq. From there I was rescued and kidnapped again and taken to Russia."

"Why were you kidnapped, are you famous?"

"It was a simple case of mistaken identity."

"Then you decided to escape by boat."

"I was kidnapped again by the same people who kidnapped me in Iran and I felt that three cases of mistaken identity were too much so I decided to escape and come to Turkey which is a more sensible country."

"Of course."

He decided to ask some questions of his own.

"Where is this boat headed?"

"Istanbul."

"Will you contact the US Embassy and release me when you get there?"

"No, we have to verify your story. It sounds improbable to me; you say you were kidnapped three times and you have no idea why."

Stewart tried not to show his disappointment as he thought his explanation was a good one, and he had not divulged anything about the real reason for being on the boat. He needed to get word to the US Embassy or Coltrane who he felt would rescue him. He was locked in a cabin and he lay on a bunk to rest, he felt it had gone reasonably well. He must have dozed off as he was awakened by the sound of the door being unlocked, the officer who had questioned him and an armed rating entered the cabin.

"Ah, Mr Hardy you are awake, I have some news for you. We are not going to Istanbul we have been diverted to a local port where we will be met by a helicopter that will transport you to Ankara."

"That sounds positive."

The officer raised his eyebrows.

"If some of your story was not true now would be the time to think about it. The message came from the National Intelligence Agency, we know them as MIT, they are our Secret Service. We dock in twenty minutes and we have been told to place you in handcuffs. They don't want you wandering off."

It was with a sinking feeling that he realised that they knew who he was. The helicopter was civilian registered and very smart, and was not what he expected, two well-dressed men were waiting beside the steps.

"Mr Hardy, pleasure to meet you sir." He was tall and very fit looking, Stewart decided that he would not like to tangle with him. He did not state his rank but said something to the guards who removed his handcuffs. While issuing this command he let his jacket swing open to reveal a holstered handgun.

The helicopter was quiet, and they could converse easily.

"I am Yusuf, is this your first visit to Turkey?"

"It is, I understand there is plenty to see here."

"You might not get sufficient time."

While they were talking Stewart was able to see between the two pilots who were sitting in front of them. There was an instrument that showed which direction they were heading. It showed a figure of one hundred and ninety degrees, which would be approximately the direction of Ankara, his aircraft navigation knowledge was helping for the first time. The flight lasted less than an hour during which they flew over a large city which he took to be Ankara, the capital of Turkey. They flew on for a further ten minutes before landing on the parade ground at what appeared to be an Army camp.

"Mr Hardy, I have a decision to make, do I put you in handcuffs or will you give me your word that you will not try to escape." As he spoke, he opened his jacket again to show the handgun.

"I have been instructed that if you try to escape, I am to shoot you in the legs, they want you alive."

Stewart looked out of the window at the armed soldiers that had appeared.

"Have they been told the same thing?"

He received a nod and a smile.

"You have my word."

The pilots did not stop the engine and they had to duck under the rotor when they left the aircraft. It was only a short walk to the nearest building, as they did so the helicopter lifted off.

"I can see that you are wondering about this place."

"Not really."

He was not interested; it was part of the Turkish secret service and that was all that mattered. He was looking around so that he could understand the layout.

"This was an Army base, but they needed more space, so they built a larger one outside the city. We, MIT, took it over and completely refurbished it. We still have our city centre offices and this is like an annex."

"There are still soldiers here?"

"Yes, they guard us and stop people trying to break out, originally, they were to stop people breaking in, but nobody has tried that. It seems that people don't break into intelligence agency facilities."

He was laughing while explaining that escaping was not possible.

"This was the officers club; you will live here unless we change our mind and put you in a cell."

"What do you mean 'live here'?"

"It is likely that you will be here for some time, some visitors who stay here are placed in cells, but we choose to treat you differently. Unless of course you become difficult."

The room was comfortable and came with room service, this was provided by a young woman who was waiting for them.

"This is Ivanna, she will take care of your room, and your laundry, she will bring you your meals and anything else you require. Incidentally, she does not speak English."

"If she does not speak English how do I tell her what I want to eat."

"You don't have a choice, if she needs to speak to you, she will call the guard at the end of the corridor, there is one on duty all day or night."

Ivanna checked the bathroom and went to leave, Stewart called out to her.

"I like your tits."

She flinched and looked at him obviously not sure how to respond, Yusuf laughed.

"Very clever Mr Hardy, she speaks good English."

"So she is not a maid, she is an intelligence officer."

He shrugged and smiled; he did that often.

"I will talk in the morning, get a good night's rest."

Chapter forty.

Turkey.

His captors had thoughtfully provided some beer and soft drinks so he poured himself a glass of orange juice and settled himself in a chair so that he could analyse his situation. He did not feel threatened, they were not violent, at least not so far. That could easily change when they interrogated him. What troubled him most was that nobody knew where he was. If Coltrane is searching for him, he would not know about the farm or that he had escaped in a boat and definitely would not know that he had been picked up at sea by a Turkish Navy vessel. Then the helicopter ride would ensure that his trail was completely lost, now he was in a MIT facility and they would not notify the US Embassy. He had completely disappeared, which led him to question what he would tell them. If he told them the true story, they definitely would not acknowledge where he was, but being forced to work for them meant he would have to have access to a computer.

One thing that the Turks were not aware of was that he did not have a copy of the software, Rula had kept complete control of the two copies that the Syrians had obtained. He could convince the Turks that he could download one from Boeing and in doing so provide the CIA with the means to locate him. It was not possible to simply download a copy and things would turn nasty when the Turks realised that. The more he thought about it he came to the decision that it would be better if he stuck to the Michael Hardy story. He would not elaborate on what he had already told them, he had flown to Tehran from Washington State and lived in an apartment in Renton. He could use his old address that he had used before he moved in with Alistair, he recognised whatever he said they could disprove it using agents that must operate from their embassy at Washington. The trick was to provide a link that the CIA could use to find him. He retired feeling more confident that he could convince them that he was Michael Hardy. He knew that they did not have the means to disprove that and any attempts to investigate Michael Hardy would alert the CIA.

He was up, washed and dressed before Ivanna tapped on his door, she wheeled in a trolly with a continental breakfast, she even said "Good Morning" in English. Before leaving she checked the laundry basket, which was empty, he was wearing the only clothes that he had, he did not say anything but hoped she would bring him some more. He had just finished his breakfast when there was a second tap on the door, it was Yusuf.

"Morning, can I join you?"

His timing was so good that Stewart suspected that the room was under observation, he would find the camera when he was alone.

"Tell me about the boat, it belongs to a property developer who has a place north of Sochi. We have been watching it from time to time as it crossed the Black Sea to Romania. What was it being used for and were you part of that operation?"

"I don't know who you are referring to, I explained that I was kidnapped by some Russians and escaped from them and ended up at the coast. I found a boat tied up at a jetty and borrowed it. On the boat were some maps and from them I identified that I was on the Black Sea. I could also see

111

that if I sailed due west for twenty or thirty miles and the turned south the next land that I would see was Turkey, I would avoid Georgia."

"Are you a sailor?"

"Not really, I've been on boats on the Puget Sound, that's near Seattle."

"Can you describe your captors?"

"Which ones, the first where Syrians, typical Arabs, the Russians all look alike to me, mostly rough military types. I don't know their names."

"That's two lots, you said you were kidnapped three times what nationality were the third lot?"

"They were Syrians, the same ones who kidnapped me the first time."

"They were operating in Russia?"

"Looks that way."

"The Russians and the Syrians cooperate in Syria, so it is possible they cooperate in Russia itself."

"No idea, I am a travel writer and h and I leave that political stuff to others. All I know is that it was a big mistake coming to this part of the world at this time."

"What do you photograph?"

"Mainly buildings, old ones which I supply to magazines and publicity companies."

"Tell me the name of some of those agencies."

"You will have heard of Photolist and Pixelview."

"No."

"Well they each have a million photographs available from their website, taken by photographers all over the world."

"Some are yours?"

"Yes, but I decided to publish my own book of photographs."

"What of?"

"Religious buildings."

"So you would be planning to come here to Turkey?"

"Absolutely Turkey has some of the most stunning religious buildings in the world."

"Sounds good, so why did they kidnap you?"

"I have absolutely no idea, I thought at first they were robbers, they took my photographic equipment.

They mistook me for somebody else, but those Syrians started a chain of events whereby others thought I was important enough to kidnap. They were all wrong."

Further discussion was interrupted by a tap on the door, it was Ivanna with his lunch. They had been talking all morning without realising it. Yusuf stood up and stretched.

"I'll leave you to your lunch we might talk again later."

As he left it occurred to Stewart that he had not done a bad job with his story. Yusuf did not appear later that day or the next two days after that, Ivanna found him a couple of old paperbacks in English to pass the time. Unfortunately, they were love stories but in the absence of anything else he forced himself to read them. They were very prudish in their descriptions of sex, so he checked the dates inside the covers, they were twelve years old. While reading he found his mind occasionally went back to his discussion with Yusuf, firstly he wished he had said some other things. Then he decided that was the story and he would stick it, no elaborating. Ivanna had brought him some clothes and laundered his own but even though they were often alone he never made any attempt to converse with her. As she seemed to have made the same decision, he assumed it was because she knew there was a hidden camera and a microphone, he did not find them.

Yusuf appeared on the fourth day, as on the first occasion there was a tap on the door as he finished his breakfast. He seemed to be in a good mood.

"Hi, I was not sure if you would be in, can we talk?"

"I'll check my diary."

"We've checked your story and as far as we can tell it is plausible, so we have made a decision. We are handing you over to your embassy."

Stewart could not believe it; they were delivering him by car to the embassy which was not far away.

"Thank you" was all he could say.

Later that day he was put in a car with Yusuf and driven the short distance to the US embassy. On arrival they got out of the car and walked in together Yusuf said something to the receptionist and walked out. He was left standing there wondering what was happening until a US Marine asked him if he needed help. The embassy staff did not know who he was or where he had come from, it was almost as though he had come directly from the coastguard ship to the embassy. The marine called a civilian who produced a form for him to fill in.

"The man who brought you here said the Turkish Coastguard had picked you up from a small boat and that you had no papers but claimed to be American, that was all he said. Can we start with your name?"

"Michael Hardy."

"Michael Hardy, we had a message about you."

They were joined by two other men and they moved to the Ambassadors office who was holding a sheet of paper.

"Mr Hardy welcome, this is a message from a CIA agent, Spencer Coltrane who instructs us to contact him if you should turn up here or if we receive any information about your whereabouts. We are further instructed to take good care of you, and nobody is to have access to you. I have sent the message, but it is one o'clock in the morning in Washington, so we won't get a reply from agent Coltrane until this afternoon at the earliest."

"I can wait."

"We have a guest room that you can use, do you need anything to eat?

"I'm OK for now."

He was taken up two floor levels and shown into a comfortable room, where he collapsed into a comfortable chair, he felt safer than he had done for weeks. The feeling was interrupted by the sudden appearance of the Ambassador and a Marine.

"We have a reply already." He was waving a paper to emphasise what he was saying.

"Agent Coltrane will be here tomorrow; in the meantime we are to keep you in guarded secure accommodation with no visitors. He goes on to say that we are not to release any information about you being here and that we should take security at the embassy very seriously."

He indicated the Marine, "There will be two Marines outside your door at all times."

Stewart slumped back in the chair, he felt even safer.

Chapter forty-one.

Ankara, Turkey.

There was a knock on his door which opened before he could reach it. Coltrane was standing there with a grin on his face.

"Agent Coltrane what kept you?"

"I came as quick as I could but since I got back, I have been followed everywhere."

"Who by?"

"Three different lots, possibly Russian, Iranian and Chinese."

"Chinese, are they involved now?"

"They obviously think I will lead them to you."

"And have you?"

"I travelled here by a military Gulfstream, that's a ten-seater, it was allegedly going to Egypt but diverted to here."

"Do you think you have lost them?"

"Not a chance, how are you?"

"Good considering, except for being a nervous wreck."

"I never thanked you for saving my life on the train, do you think that woman, what was she called would have shot me?"

"Rula, without any hesitation."

"When you asked her, she let me go, have you had a relationship with her?

"Sadly no, she is too young."

"Rubbish."

Stewart changed the subject.

"What's the plan."

"I have to get you out of here and back to Washington as quickly as possible without anybody realising I have done it."

Stewart studied his face.

"Does anybody know I am here?"

"It would be easy for me to say 'no' but I think we have to assume 'yes'. I told the Ambassador here not to let any information about you to leave this building, but I expect it has."

"So this embassy is being watched."

"We don't know that, so we are going to make a fast escape. The Gulfstream that brought me here is parked at Ankara airport, it is refuelled and ready to go. There is a detachment of Marines here at the embassy, they provide security."

"I have met some of them."

"We will use six of them as our security when we leave in two identical cars. Four Marines will be in the first car and we will be in the second car with two Marines, we will be dressed as Marines. If we are stopped the first car will deal with the Police or Turkish Army or whoever stops us and tell them the second car has Marines in it as well. Hopefully, they will wave it through."

"Where will we be going?"

Coltrane had an exasperated look.

"To the airport of course to collect a diplomatic package from the Gulfstream."

"Have we got two identical cars?"

"Hertz are delivering them."

"Sounds workable."

Stewart was getting used to how government forces worked. They went down to the basement where there were six Marines waiting for them. Coltrane gave them precise instructions which were mainly to do with pushing hard for people to get out of their way. Two sets of Marine clothing, including steel helmets and weaponry appeared and Coltrane and himself changed into it. Nobody from the Embassy staff were there and when he mentioned this to Coltrane he replied.

"I haven't told them what we are doing, it could leak out even before we leave."

Outside were two SUV's, they looked new, Coltrane commented on this and one of the Marines muttered.

"Let's hope they look like that when we return them."

Coltrane smiled. "Luckily, we have diplomatic immunity."

They climbed into the SUV's, he along with Coltrane were in the rear seat of the second car as they pulled out of the Embassy entrance and turned in in the direction of the airport. The two cars were close together and driving at speed, faster than Stewart was happy with but he did not say anything. The airport was thirty miles from the Embassy which should have taken them about sixty minutes but due to the fast driving they encountered airport signs in half that time. The airport was in sight when as they left a roundabout, they encountered a roadblock of police cars and were forced to stop. The front seat passenger in their car who was armed with a sub-machine gun produced a handgun which he cradled on his lap. Coltrane did not look nervous, but he instructed Stewart to do nothing.

"We are all US citizens with diplomatic cover, they can't interfere with our free movement."

The discussion with the front car ended and the police cars moved out of the way, one pulled in front of them and another followed them. Both had their sirens on and blue lights flashing, Coltrane was laughing.

"It looks as though they are escorting us to the airport."

He was right, they overtook all the traffic and turned into the airport entrance and onto a road that took them to a large hanger. There was a red and white barrier which was lifted as they approached and on the other side, they were joined by an Airport Security car which led them to the aircraft. There were soldiers from the Turkish Army on duty guarding the aircraft. The cars pulled up at the steps and everybody got out, the police and the Marines were shaking hands as Coltrane led him up the steps.

"Take you kit off and give it to one of the Marines, we don't need it anymore."

Coltrane had spoken briefly to the driver of the first car who told him that we had been reported for driving too fast, so the police had decided to stop them. He had waved his diplomatic immunity card and the police offered to escort them, so he accepted.

Chapter forty-two.

Washington.

The aircraft was spacious and the seats comfortable and arranged so that two passengers faced each other with a table between them. They sat near the back of the cabin on the right, additional crew members sat on the left. Stewart breathed out and relaxed.

"I'm beginning to feel safe, at last."

The cabin door closed and there was activity in the cockpit, in minutes both engines started and soon after that they moved forward. Coltrane had made the journey out from Washington and knew what to expect.

"The flight will take fifteen hours including a stop at the Azores for fuel and a burger, it's nearly mid-day here so allowing for the time difference we will be in Washington by early morning tomorrow, that's local time."

The cockpit door was open, and they could see out of the windscreen as they taxied onto the runway which was covered in black rubber skid marks. Stewart shifted in his seat so that he could get a good view of the take-off, a new experience for him. Unfortunately one of the crew shut the door, it was probably a safety measure. The take-off was smooth and after they levelled off coffee appeared, and they started to review the situation. Coltrane was up to speed on everything except the details of the journey across Russia.

"I am sure that you realise that it isn't over yet. When we reach Washington it will restart, the same people will be after you."

"You are right of course but it will seem better in the good old USA."

Stewart was faced with hours of either sleeping or talking to Coltrane who seemed to have opted for sleep. As they settled down Coltrane pointed upwards.

"Stack of magazines in that overhead locker, I read them all on the way out."

They landed at the Azores where the weather was best described as fresh, the wind was blowing off the Atlantic. The aircrew thought a big storm was on the way so after a quick snack they were back in the air. Stewart was surprised when he was woken up and asked to put on his seat belt ready for landing, At Ronald Regan Airport they taxied into a hanger which was guarded by the Army and they were told to stay in the aircraft until the hanger doors were closed.

Stewart was realistic. "At some time I am going to have to come out into the open."

"Not until we are certain it is safe."

"It will never be safe, even if I had trained more operators, I will still be someone who can do what they ask and if they realise that I have tampered with the software then I will be even more important to them. Now my safety lies in being just that, the only one who can help, nobody can risk hurting me. What's the next move?"

"We have decided to go back to the original arrangement of three CIA agents guarding you at your apartment except you will work there. That cuts out the dangerous part when you travel from the apartment to your office."

"Will those three agents be enough?"

"Definitely not, the whole estate will be secured by the Army, nobody will get close to you."

It sounded great but Stewart was not looking forward to being locked up in that way.

Coltrane moved on to the practicalities.

"What do you have to do first, train new operators or secure the programme. Incidentally are we still locked out of it?"

"We can use the programme as it was originally intended. While I was being forced to work on it in Iraq and Russia, I changed many things without letting anybody know. I need to install the new security measures that I talked about and they are mostly ready to install. I did that at our offices before I left Washington."

"So how long?"

"Two days possibly, three at the most, then I can start training. Where will we do that?"

"At our offices, we are clearing some vegetation so a light helicopter can land, it will ferry you back and to without exposing you to the risk of travelling by road. The security at our office will be beefed up so that when you land in the car park you will be safe. While in the air your helicopter will have another alongside that is state of the art."

Stewart thought he could not argue with any of that, but first he had to get to his apartment. He found himself in a convoy of SUV's with motorcycle outriders that took less than fifteen minutes to reach the apartment. The first person he saw when he exited the lift was Rosie Cooke, the CIA agent who had been part of his protection team.

"Rosie, it's good to see you are the others still here?"

"Aaron and Darren are outside. We have been here since you left, keeping the place secure ready for your return. Is there anything I can get you?"

"Not at present I just need to shower, some clean clothes and to relax."

Coltrane had decided to do the same and as he moved to the door his phone rang which brought him to attention. He mouthed "President" to them and moved into a corner to take the call, it was a long one.

"That was the President, he welcomes you back and was checking that you are being looked after. He wants to talk with you when you have settled back in, I am to make a time for the meeting. I will be here in the morning to get things started; you will find all the computer things that you need in one of the bedrooms. You can play with them until I get back."

Stewart felt better after his shower and a change of clothes and he began to unbox the computer hardware.

"Another day, another place, another computer set up, life is predictable."

He was in familiar surroundings and settled down, Rosie provided good meals and he could sleep in his own bed, the nightmares of the previous weeks faded. Coltrane appeared every day but did not interfere with his progress. The helicopter had arrived, and the pilots checked the landing area before disappearing to their base, he could call it anytime he needed it.

Chapter forty-three.

Strangely the meeting with the President had been arranged for a Sunday morning, Stewart had no idea why this was so but presumed that somebody had a good reason. The city centre was busy, but the White House was eerily quiet, there were staff working away but noticeably the offices with names on the doors were in darkness. He mentioned this to Coltrane who was puzzled.

"I think this is going to be one of those meetings that never took place."

This seemed to be confirmed when they found the room for the meeting, it was an informal waiting room and the only person there was the President himself.

"Come in and sit down, we are on our own today." There was a steaming coffee machine on a table which he pointed to.

"We have to look after ourselves this morning, I like that very much; you can get too much attention."

"Tell me about your adventures, please take your time as I need to know everything."

It took more than an hour due to the number of questions. When he had finished Stewart sat back, he was not sure what would happen next.

"So we have total control of this system again, nobody else can use it?"

"I've changed the security arrangements so that it is now totally secure."

"Tell me how it will work."

"I will be training four new operators who will be based at different locations, they will each have their own passwords. To start using the program two of them will need to log in at roughly the same time and both will need to enter an authorisation code that is provided by yourself Mr President."

"Bit like the red phone that we currently use for authorising the use of nuclear weapons."

"That's it."

"So there are only four people and yourself who can use this system?"

"I will not be able to use it. For somebody to take control they will have to abduct two operators and get authorisation from yourself."

"Very clever, so taking you prisoner is not an option."

"That's correct, I don't want to be hunted for the rest of my life in the way I have for the last few weeks."

"Have you advised anybody of that fact?"

"No, but I will. I intend to retire; I am a multi-millionaire, unfortunately my brother was killed but had made a will naming me as his heir, so I have no need to work for Boeing or the CIA. Agent Coltrane will make sure that the people that matter realise I am no longer able to help."

"Which people?"

"Those that wanted to take control of the system, and maybe others who were thinking along the same lines."

"But none have any definite information."

Coltrane was shaking his head, so Stewart joined him.

"When does this new security arrangement become effective.?"

"Later this month."

"Until then you are till at risk."

"I'm hoping Coltrane here will take good care of me."

The President sat still for a minute and seemed to reach a decision.

"What I am about to say to you now will not be repeated by you to anybody and if you do, I will deny that I said it or that this meeting took place. Is that clearly understood?"

Stewart and Coltrane spoke together. "Yes."

The President was choosing his words carefully.

"This remote-control system is a marvellous tool for controlling world peace but if the wrong people had got control of it there would have been a disastrous situation. Fortunately, thanks to your intervention they did not so we are able to make full use of it and I have decided that is what we will do. You will remember the first contact from Global Action, they had targeted all the nuclear armed countries with the instruction to take all their nuclear weapons out of service. Most of the governments agreed after lengthy discussion, except for North Korea, they only agreed when two aircraft blocked runways in their country. Well I can tell you now that while we have partially complied, the others have not. Some countries claimed that they had started on the decommissioning but are still debating or stalling and North Korea never did anything. We are missing a big opportunity to rid the world of nuclear weapons."

He took a deep breath and carried on.

"Stewart, I want you to take control of a number of aircraft and land them on the runways of the most important airfields of each of those countries including ourselves. I understand that with the engines running nobody will approach them and they will stay there until the fuel runs out."

Stewart and Coltrane were mentally checking that they had heard him correctly, Stewart recovered first.

"You included us, the United States."

He wished he had not spoken because he was beginning to understand what the plan was, but the President answered.

"If we did not include ourselves it would be telling the governments of all countries that we were responsible. More importantly it gives me the opportunity to be indignant and go public so that nobody, worldwide, will be in any doubt as to what is happening. They will be certain that a terrorist group were behind the whole demonstration".

Stewart realised it was very risky but clever, but the President carried on.

"If ten days after these incidents there is still no proof of action having been taken to de-commission the nuclear weapons a second demonstration will take place. A departing airliner will overfly the capital of the offending country or countries at low altitude before returning to its departure airfield. No government should be in any doubt that they need to comply and show that all their nuclear weapons have been taken out of service and de-activated."

Coltrane was smiling.

"Brilliant plan, no damage to buildings and nobody will have been hurt."

The President was leaning forward and carried on.

"Not then, but that could change if any country still does not comply. Ten days later the final message would be delivered."

"Which is?"

"Three aircraft will be flown into the most important buildings of any country that has failed to comply. They will still be certain that a well-funded and organised terrorist group is in control".

Stewart and Coltrane looked at each other, Stewart recovered first.

"Mr President, I'm not sure if I could do all that you have suggested."

"Why ever not?"

"Because no warlike act would have been committed by any country, the final message would be an act of war."

"Rubbish, you would be preventing a warlike act, think of the bigger picture."

"I am thinking of the bigger picture, and I don't like it."

"Are you telling me that you won't act if your President tells you to?"

"Of course I will have to consider my position if I get an executive order to do as you suggest."

"So what is the point of a quiet meeting here if we go and publicise it afterwards."

"I see your point Mr President but if this all goes wrong, I will get all the blame."

"I understand and I don't want that to happen, will you do the first parts, take control and put the aircraft on the runways and then do the low flight past?"

"I do need to think about this, it is a bit of a shock to learn of your plans. I must make it clear that I will not be party to a plan to kill a couple of thousand innocent people, that would be a terrible action."

There was silence in the room as each person thought about what had been said. The President reached into his brief case and produced a satellite phone which he handed to Coltrane.

"This is how we will communicate about this business; this phone is untraceable. When we have completed this exercise it will be destroyed. You can work out how best to target the countries which have not complied. I will advise you which they are and then you can proceed in any order that you wish but please take less than ten days. I understand that you will not need to use the other operators or get authorisation cades my me, is that correct?"

Stewart nodded and the President stood up and thanked them both for their co-operation and once again insisted that the meeting had never taken place.

Stewart found that he was shaking when they left the building.

"I'm not happy with this situation. Only you and I know of the meeting, the President can always deny such a plan was never his idea."

Coltrane was also beginning to feel concerned. "You can do what he asks without any help? The first two tasks should be straightforward and nobody gets killed."

"Yes, but you notice how quickly he moved away from any further discussion of the final option. I feel sure that he intends to return to it after the first two have been completed and there are still governments that have not complied with the demands and then I will be vulnerable. I knew these sorts of things went on in politics, but I've never encountered them myself."

"Cheer up, it's Sunday and it's a nice bright sunny day, we'll get ourselves a beer."

They found their security detail and advised them of the plan and went to a small bar not far from the White House and ordered two beers, the smell of food was overpowering, and Stewart suddenly felt hungry.

"Have you got any plans for Sunday lunch?"

"No I live on my own."

Stewart realised that he knew nothing about Coltrane.

"No wife?"

"She left me; I'm divorced."

He was a bit surprised as Coltrane was always smartly dressed in a well pressed suit, clean shirt and a bright tie, standard CIA uniform.

"We'll eat here."

"What about our security men? Shall we ask them to join us?"

Coltrane looked horrified.

"They won't do that, but I'll nip out and tell them they can come in and eat here, on their own if they wish."

He went off to find them and Stewart turned slowly to study the diners and was astonished to see Rula, the Syrian sitting at a table with three other diners. She was looking at him and made a slow mock salute with her right hand. Coltrane appeared at his side.

"I've spoken to the waiter; we have a table at the back of the room."

Stewart was about to object until he noticed Rula and her friends had stood up and were leaving. She blew him a kiss as she passed. Coltrane noticed and mentioned it as they sat down.

"Pretty that one, is she an old friend?"

"That's Rula Asad, she is with Qasad, the Syrian terrorist group. You saw her on the train in Russia, she was the one who pushed you into the compartment".

Coltrane was shocked. "Bloody hell, what's she doing here?"

"Should not be difficult to guess."

"When did you last see her?"

"Several weeks ago in Russia."

"I'll deal with it."

Stewart was worried and said so.

"How have they found me so quickly?"

"Easy, you were living in Washington and now you are back in Washington."

"Yes but how did they know about today's meeting here?"

"They did not know, it was just luck, they were having a meal and so were we. I said I will deal with it and I will." He was on the phone to Lewis who was still in the car outside.

Stewart was not so sure that it had been just luck that Rula and her associates just happened to be in the bar where they went to eat. He knew that she was far more organised and that he was probably being watched and was followed to the White House and his security detail had not noticed.

Once back at his apartment and he felt strangely safe to be in his own environment with plenty of security. Rosie was waiting for him.

"I'll not ask you if you want something to eat, I heard you ate at a swish place near the White House."

The guards had obviously reported in.

"It was not swish, but I enjoyed it. Have you been told that some of the people who were involved in my kidnap were also in the bar?"

"Yes, we will be more vigilant in future but suggest that you remain inside the apartment until the matter is contained."

Stewart sighed, a prisoner once again.

Chapter Forty-four.

Stewart was up early next morning, had his breakfast and started to work on how he could comply with the President's requests. He knew it would take some time to bypass the new security measures that he had already put in place. Coltrane appeared earlier than usual with some news.

"After we parted yesterday, I rang Crowe, you may remember him he was the agent in Baltimore who kept check on the Syrians."

"I remember, hundreds of them he said."

"That was everywhere, all States. He usually watched twenty or so, well after that business at the house there which we paid for and where you were kidnapped, the Syrian group stopped using it."

"I never understood why we paid for it".

"We are allied to the rebels in Syria, Russia is allied to the government, but the real reason is that by providing a nice big house we knew where they were. After that raid they moved out and a group of them left the country, that could be the people who took you away. Crowe told me that different people came into the country and stayed in smaller groups, four to a house which they rented themselves. Mostly they claim they are here for cultural reasons but almost all are here for other reasons. Four came in together a week ago and it is obvious that they are a unit, and they managed to disappear. It took a few days to find out where they are living, we now know that they are here in Washington. A decision was made to deport them. In fact Crowe told me that most of the Syrians are being deported but when he decided about the four in the Washington house, he realised that the female was not there. We know that wherever she goes a young lad always goes with her and he is still there so Crowe thinks she will reappear. The lad is called Emir Juda, they are both members of Qasad the terrorist group. When I told him we had seen the woman, Rula Asad, who you recognised he was delighted. He will let us know when there are developments."

He left in a cheerful mood which Stewart did not share, he was still worried about what had been said at the meeting at the White House. He did not see Coltrane for a couple of days but when he reappeared, he was in a good mood.

"I've got good news for you, two lots of good news. Firstly the Syrian woman known as Rula that we talked about turned up at the address here in Washington and she and the other three were picked up and are being deported."

Stewart felt it was a temporary respite as the Syrians seemed to be able to enter the country any time they wanted to.

"Secondly, I had a call this morning from the President, he said you are not to take any action on what we discussed at that meeting. Don't do anything except inform him when the new updated version of the software is ready to use and what procedure has been set in place."

"Did he say why?"

"Something has changed but he did not say what it was, that's politics for you. He probably leaked his plans and someone, security or the military have made him change his mind. As you were not happy with his instructions, I now assume you are relieved."

"Very."

"What are you going to do with yourself?"

"I had been thinking about the future while I was away, plenty of time to think and decide what I want to do with the rest of my life. I feel that I have been given another chance after what happened to Ray and my brother. I will resign from my job and probably move away from Washington. I will sell Alistair Investments as there have been several good offers. I plan to spend more time flying."

"Where will you live?"

"Not sure but I have seen details of places where you can have a house on the edge of an airfield, have your own hangar and fly whenever the weather is right. I may even learn to fly a powered aircraft which would give me a new challenge. Other than that maybe so some fishing and who know even find a wife!"

Coltrane smiled. "Lots of ideas and I expect you will begin to make changes now that your work here is finished. I wish you all the best and will shake hands as it has been good working alongside you even when things were difficult. We probably won't meet again."

Stewart smiled and thanked him for all his help and as Coltrane left the apartment Stewart wondered when they would meet again.

ENDS

If you enjoyed this book you might find other *James A Jones* thrillers interest you. James has written many books that are about different subjects.
These include:

We lost democracy

First strike

Domination

Eighteen days

Final mission

Smart control

Total control

Polyhedron

Go to www.jamesajones.co.uk/blog for more information.

Printed in Great Britain
by Amazon